FOR DESIRE ALONE

MISTRESS MATCHMAKER BOOK 2

JESS MICHAELS

For Desire Alone
Mistress Matchmaker Book 2

For more information, contact Jess Michaels

www.AuthorJessMichaels.com

To contact the author:

Email: Jess@AuthorJessMichaels.com

Twitter www.twitter.com/JessMichaelsBks

Facebook: www.facebook.com/JessMichaelsBks

Jess Michaels raffles a gift certificate EVERY month to members of her newsletter, so sign up on her website: http://www.authorjessmichaels.com/

For everyone who helped me remember who I am again, especially Michael (who never forgot). Thank you for the love, support and belief that carried me through a very long, dark night.

CHAPTER 1

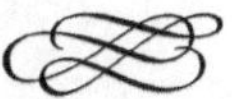

"Miss Desmond," the solicitor sniffed as he shuffled the paperwork on his desk. Just as he had all afternoon, he refused to look at her. "I really *don't* know what else to tell you. As I've explained at length, Lord Heathcote's final settlements are very clear. He *did* gift you the sum of one thousand pounds and there are the other details, but beyond that, there is nothing."

Mariah leaned back in the uncomfortable chair across the desk from the weasel of a man who now held her fate, her future...or rather, her lack thereof...in his hands. Her ears rang and her vision blurred as what he had been repeating for over half an hour sank into her consciousness.

She had nothing.

"But—but," she stammered. "Owen and I..." She stopped and corrected herself. "The earl and I had a longstanding relationship. I was led to believe that there were to be arrangements made for me."

The solicitor pursed his lips. It was evident he knew exactly what kind of "relationship" Mariah and Owen had shared for three years. More evident was how little he approved and thought of her. But that she was accustomed to. Mistresses were hardly seen as human by most in good Society.

Only Owen had never treated her so low. He'd seen her as a partner, almost a spouse...or so he'd always claimed. More to the point, he had promised that she would never again have to find a protector if he were to die before she did.

Those promises had been made in the dark, while they lay in each other's arms. So in her mind, Owen had been different from all the other men who simply used and discarded their mistresses.

Now she wasn't so certain and her doubts in him wounded her and made her feel a deep sense of guilt.

"There *were* arrangements made for you," the solicitor snapped as he flipped his ledger book shut. "One thousand pounds. And whatever little baubles the earl bought for you are to remain with you. You will be allowed to remain in your townhome for six months without paying for its use, unless you find another...*understanding* for yourself during that period. Your servants have been paid for their wages through that point as well. Honestly, Miss Desmond, you should be happy the earl made an arrangement for a woman such as you at all."

Mariah flinched. *A woman such as herself.* A whore, he meant. But she had never felt like a whore. She had never felt like a mistress with Owen. Until now. Now when it was clear he hadn't cared enough for her to provide any kind of solid future. Despite everything they had shared.

She sucked in a breath and tried to fight the tears that stung behind her eyes.

Tried and failed, for one trickled down her cheek despite her best efforts.

The solicitor shifted with disgust and discomfort at her emotional display. He lunged to his feet. "There is nothing more to be said about it. The money shall be deposited into your account and be accessible to you today. Now good day."

He motioned toward the door, his mouth a thin, grim line. With a shudder, Mariah stood and straightened her shoulders in the hopes she could exit with some small shred of dignity intact. With her head held high and tears continuing to stream down her cheeks, she strode past the man and left his office without a goodbye or a glance behind her.

He slammed the door just at her heels and left her standing in the hallway with an equally disgusted servant in wait for her departure.

She made her way to her carriage and found her driver holding the door for her. Potts was such a friendly face after the previous half hour's unkindness that she could have hugged him. Especially when he seemed so concerned by her demeanor that he wordlessly took a clean handkerchief from his pocket and handed it to her after he helped her into the vehicle.

She nodded her thanks as she wiped her eyes.

"Home, miss?" Potts asked.

She shook her head. *Home.* Christ, that place wasn't home anymore, was it? She would lose it too soon to call it a home.

"No," she managed past a thick tongue. "I would like to pay a visit to Miss Manning."

He nodded and closed the door. He didn't need to ask for more detail than that—after all, Mariah's best friend was Vivien Manning. They made this trip once a week at minimum. And though she looked forward to seeing her friend during this time of trial, there was also a part of her which dreaded the meeting. Vivien was sure to have a great deal to say on the subject of her future. Her friend was nothing if not opinionated on the subject of mistresses and protectors.

And Mariah wasn't certain she wanted to hear it all.

"One thousand pounds?" Vivien repeated blankly, setting her tea aside to stare at Mariah. Her shock and her pity were painted across her face.

The heat of humiliation burned Mariah's cheeks, but she

managed to nod.

"Yes," she whispered. "And the house and servants for six months. And the jewelry, of course."

"Still…" Vivien shook her head. "That is a pittance. Do you have any savings from what he gave you over your time together?"

Mariah nodded slowly. "I have a bit of savings from my pin money over the years, but it isn't much."

Vivien arched a brow. "Not to be indelicate, my dear, but how much is 'not much'?"

Mariah shifted. "A little more than five hundred pounds." When Vivien flinched, Mariah rushed to explain herself. "Owen took care of all my needs during our time together and he highly encouraged me to spend my pin money. Since he promised I would be taken care of…" She trailed off. "Well, I never bothered to set much aside in case of this kind of circumstance."

Vivien nodded, but Mariah could see she was only being placating. "I can understand that. But your troubles remain, don't they? You cannot survive more than a year or two at most with that sum. Perhaps three if you sell the jewelry."

Vivien had just voiced Mariah's deepest terrors and her throat seemed to close with panic. "Yes," she whispered. "That is my assessment as well."

Vivien's eyes narrowed and she slapped her palm on the low table between them. "Dear God, you gave that man three years of your life. I know you would have given him twenty more if he asked."

She could bear no more. Mariah put her hands over her face and began to cry. Vivien *tsked* softly but moved to the settee beside her friend and wrapped an arm around her. Mariah pressed her face into Vivien's shoulder and sobbed out all her pain and betrayal for a few moments. Finally, she pulled herself back together and sat up straighter.

"I'm sorry," she said with a shake of her head. "Everything is just so discombobulated. First, Owen dies in that awful fire."

She hesitated as a burst of sharp, horrible pain gripped her. She hated to think of Owen trapped by flame. In terrible pain and equal fear in his last moments. Every time she did, she felt sick.

She swallowed back bile and continued, "Then to discover that everything he told me about his arrangements wasn't done. It is all such a shock."

Vivien shook her head. "Poor Owen did not deserve to die so terribly, I agree. But as for the arrangements, I can spare him no sympathy. He clearly never intended to fulfill his promises to you."

"No!" Mariah burst out. She might believe a great many things, but not this. "That cannot be true. He had no idea he would die so young. He must have merely been putting off the protections he promised me during our affair without realizing he would be taken so soon."

Vivien bit back a bark of humorless laughter. "If he had made *no* arrangement whatsoever, I could believe that to be true, but he did make some rather pitiful overtures to 'protect' you after his death. Why not make the full arrangements instead? Hell, even if he decided he would add money to that fund for you in the future, a thousand pounds per three years? Even if you two stayed attached for twenty years, you would only be settled with six thousand pounds. Hardly enough to live on, even modestly."

Mariah squeezed her eyes shut. Vivien was only voicing the very thoughts that had been in her own head since she left the solicitor's office. But hearing them out loud still made her want to defend Owen. Somehow.

"But he could have simply thought he had more time," she said. "He could have—"

Vivien grasped both her hands and squeezed them gently. "Why do you insist on protecting him when you know how miserly he was in his treatment of you?"

Mariah let out a long sigh. "Because I loved him."

Vivien shook her head, though she didn't seem surprised by this revelation. Mariah supposed she wasn't. Mariah had always spoken highly of her lover. She had never looked for a bigger or better man to protect her and had assumed that they would be together all their lives. It wasn't an unheard of possibility. Several men in Society had stayed with their mistresses for the entire span of their days, giving them an almost equal respect and security as they did their wives.

She and Owen had talked about long-term arrangements for her comfort, of course, but she had never assumed those plans would come into play for decades to come.

"Falling in love with him was your first mistake," Vivien said softly. "A mistress *doesn't* love her protector, nor does she expect or believe he loves her in return, no matter what he says in the height of passion. We've seen too many of our kind be hurt by such lofty expectations and wild emotions."

"Like me," Mariah said with a shuddering sigh.

Vivien gave her a sympathetic gaze but did not deny that Mariah had suddenly been deposited into the ranks of young women she and Vivien had often pitied for their foolish choices.

"So, tell me, now that you know the facts of what has been laid out for you, regardless of the reason behind them, what shall you do?" Vivien asked.

Mariah pondered that for a moment. She had never considered what her future would hold if Owen was gone. Now she was forced to do so.

"I don't know," she began, but Vivien clucked her tongue.

"Yes, you do." Her friend met her eyes and held there. Mariah dipped her chin. Of course there was only one option remaining.

"I suppose my best and only chance is to re-enter the field and hope to find a new protector," she said, though her heart wasn't in the words she spoke. "I must start over."

Vivien nodded. "Good, I'm glad you are seeing this through wide-open and reasonable eyes. Though you have a good head on your shoulders, so I never expected anything less."

"Thank you," Mariah murmured. "At some point that will be a comfort, I'm certain."

"I could assist you, you know," Vivien offered.

Mariah jerked her gaze to her friend and laughed, the first since Owen's death. "You mean put your mistress matchmaker skills to work for me?"

Vivien nodded. "Why does such a suggestion make you chuckle?" she asked. "I have been known for positive matches of this kind for some time now."

"Yes," Mariah conceded. "Very positive. Your last resulted in a marriage."

Vivien pursed her lips and looked both a little perturbed and slightly proud. After all, the recent marriage of Viscount Andrew Callis and his former mistress Lysandra Keates had caused a romantic scandal that seemed to rock Society to its very core. It remained a foremost topic of gossip.

"Well, it is a happy marriage, at least," Vivien offered weakly.

Mariah shrugged. That was true. The couple in question did, indeed, seem blissfully happy together. No unkind word could keep them from glowing whenever they entered a room together.

"A *marriage*," she repeated. "And rule one of being a mistress is never to fall in love with one's protector, yes?"

Vivien gave a conciliatory nod. "Yes, yes. Andrew and Lysandra were obviously the exception that proves that rule."

"I don't know. I think your matches might be a bit too dangerous for me, my dear."

Vivien waved off her teasing with a tiny smile. "Very well, I shall not put my matchmaking skills to use for you if you do not desire them. *But* you must come to my party tomorrow."

Mariah drew back as a burst of pain ripped through her at the very thought. "I don't know. Owen has only been dead for a few weeks. How could I come out so soon? How could I look for a lover so callously?"

Vivien gave her a look of fresh pity. "My dearest, I know you mourn him, despite his many faults. I understand why you do. But Owen himself dictated this path for you, did he not? By providing so little for you, he must have guessed you would be forced back into the path of other protectors if he died."

Mariah flinched. "I cannot deny the truth of that statement. No matter how much I wish to do so."

Vivien nodded. "If you wait until your heart has mended, you will be out of money or at least out of a home. And while you would be welcome here, of course, it is not in your best interest to look for a protector from a position of weakness and poverty. It is best to do it now before you are desperate."

Mariah nodded. "I know you are right. Very well, I will attend your ball tomorrow."

"Good!" Vivien clapped her hands together with an excitement Mariah couldn't bring herself to feel. In fact, the only sense she had at the moment was deep anxiety.

"And there will be men there tomorrow seeking new mistresses?" she asked, almost hoping for an answer in the negative.

But Vivien nodded with a grin. "Oh yes. I have had several gentlemen contact me discreetly to say that they were on the prowl. And though I promise not to push you or them toward each other since you do not wish for me to matchmake, I'm certain you will find each other on your own."

Mariah nodded. "Very well. Then the ball tomorrow it is, I suppose." She shook her head. "And I shall endeavor to be as charming a potential mistress as I can. Even if my smile pains me and my stomach churns with the thought of having a new man touch me."

Vivien touched her hand lightly. "In time, those feelings will fade, my dear, I promise you. And with the right man, you will one day enjoy your path again."

Mariah nodded as if she agreed with Vivien, but in her heart she knew both her statements were a lie. There would never be a time when this path she was on didn't hurt. And there would never be another man to make her want and care as deeply as Owen had.

It wasn't possible.

CHAPTER 2

John Rycroft was both utterly bored and pulsating with a desire that never seemed to be fully quenched. The two senses had never meshed well before. In fact, in combination they almost always resulted in trouble with cards, drink or women. Sometimes all three.

All of which were highly available to him in his current location, the London estate of the infamous Vivien Manning. He looked around him with a tiny smile and was punished for his distraction when his hostess lightly slapped his arm with her fan.

"And away you go, you naughty man," she teased. "Not even paying attention to me in the slightest. Am I so boring to you?"

He glanced at her. "Not at all, Vivien! I apologize, but your ballrooms and parlors always offer such ample diversion and amusements. I cannot help but have my mind stray."

Vivien shook her head, but it was apparent from her smile that there was no truth to her teasing. "You know, most men come here with the intention of looking for a mistress. And you come looking for a buffet of lovers instead. I hardly know what to do with you."

"No woman does, at least beyond the obvious." He chuckled, but his words rang too true for him to find real humor in them.

Vivien frowned slightly. "Have you ever even taken a mistress, John?"

He shrugged. "Why settle for one person in my bed? If I want to do that, I'll take a wife, God help us both. When it comes to pleasure, I've always preferred infinite variety."

His words were true, of course, and elicited the desired burst of laughter from Vivien and any others standing within earshot. But John could scarcely join in. There were *other* reasons he did not choose to settle down with any one woman, mistress, wife or anything else.

He could be no one's rock, no one's hero, no one's love. Something had broken in him long ago and since there was no fixing that, he simply avoided situations where someone would or could ask him for more than he could give. In the end, that only resulted in disappointment and pain.

Emotions he had washed his hands of long ago. No, he was here for pleasure. Empty, frivolous, explosive pleasure of all varieties.

"No matter what I'm searching for, this is quite the fete, my dear," he said with a smile for Vivien.

He had always liked Vivien, though he'd never taken her to his bed. Not even when she was available.

"You know I *always* throw the best parties," she said with a wide smile.

John shrugged. "You say that in a teasing fashion, but it is true. You serve the best wine, offer the luckiest card games, the finest company and the loveliest women. No wonder you are the most celebrated courtesan of the century."

He lifted his glass as if his excessive compliments were a toast, but before he could complete his ramblings he looked across the room and stopped dead in his tracks. A woman had just entered the ballroom.

Not just any woman. Mariah Desmond.

"To Vivien," one of the revelers nearby completed when he would not and the others raised their glass.

John shook off his surprise, though he could not help but continue to stare at Mariah, even as he lifted his glass to Vivien.

Dear God, but she was beautiful. Auburn hair like dark fire swept up in a complicated style that accentuated her long, pale neck and her pink cheeks. And her eyes, those hazel eyes that seemed to change with her mood, with the color of her gown, with the damn season. Witch's eyes, he had always called them, meant to cast a spell.

Vivien arched a brow as she followed his line of sight to the entryway.

"Ah, I see you have found Mariah," she said, her tone neutral and softer so the others around, who had gone back to their own conversations, wouldn't hear. "Not that I would have expected any less. You two are good friends, are you not?"

John flinched. Friends with Mariah? He supposed that was technically true. He had always been *friendly* with her. Thanks to his longstanding friendship with her late protector, the Earl of Heathcote, he had no other choice.

But that was all for show. On the inside, he felt no friendliness when it came to her. Lust, yes. Desire so keen that it pained him. And it never faded, not even when he poured it into other women.

"Yes," he choked as he watched Mariah draw a quick breath before she walked fully into the room, smiling for the ladies and gentlemen around her. "I have always called her a friend. But…what is she doing here?"

Vivien looked at him in surprise. "Were you not aware of her circumstance? You always seem to know everything of importance in our circles. Even if you didn't, you and Owen were thick as thieves, weren't you? I would think you would at least know his business better than others."

John bit his tongue to keep his first reaction from coming to the forefront. "I—yes, I admit I had heard something of what happened to Mariah after Owen's death."

That was…*partially* true, but since Vivien and Mariah were close friends, he wasn't about to say more.

Vivien shrugged. "Then you must guess her reasons for being here. Mariah has no choice but to ally herself with a new protector."

For a moment, John lost all contact with anything in the room but Mariah. He saw no one else, he heard no one else, including Vivien as she continued to talk. All he could do was stare at his best friend's former lover. A woman he had lusted after for three long years, even as he pretended to feel nothing but vague friendship toward her.

Mariah moved forward and smiled as some man gave her a drink. A titled man, no less. John could not remember his name, but he hated him at present. Her companion leaned in too close and whispered something to her. She laughed and reached up to touch the other man's arm lightly.

"Fuck," John muttered beneath his breath.

"John!" Vivien laughed, dragging him back to reality. "Such violent language, I am quite shocked."

"I doubt anyone could shock you, Vivien," he said, but his words tasted sour.

She stared at him. "Dear God, you've never left a party of mine or anyone else's on the arm of the same woman twice. Everyone knows you are a shameless libertine. Why in the world would you care what Mariah does?"

John shifted. Vivien was too wise and far too close to Mariah for him to explain the intricacies of his reaction to her friend. A reaction he could scarce explain to himself.

Instead, he shrugged.

"I *don't* care," he lied and downed the remainder of his drink in one swig. He set it on the tray of the closest footman and smiled at Vivien. "She can do as she wishes. And now I should go make my rounds. As you say, I never leave with the same woman twice and it is time for me to find tonight's lover. Good evening, Vivien."

She wrinkled her brow as he turned, but he heard her say softly, "Good evening, John."

He clenched his fists into his sides as he stomped, rather than walked through the ballroom. An anger boiled inside of him that made no sense and only rewarded him with great discomfort. He hardly wanted to consider it at all.

Except he couldn't help but do so. His gaze kept flitting back to Mariah. Now she had not one man to hold court over, but *five*. And each one was just as scandalous as John himself was known to be. They were men who would love to take her to their beds and revel in her body for a year or two. Men who had probably noticed her when she was on the arm of Owen. Admired her for her...charms. For what her lover had told them of her skills. And there she smiled and chatted flirtatiously with them all.

And that was just about enough for John.

He spun on his heel and marched toward her. As he neared her, Mariah finally tore her gaze away from her drooling companions and smiled at him. The expression lit her up like a candle from within and something inside of John stuttered.

But he shook off the reaction and instead reached for Mariah's arm.

"I need to speak to you," he barked without preamble and despite the fact that her companions stared at him in as much surprise as she did herself.

Her smile fell at his sharp tone and unexpected touch, and she lightly tugged back against him. "John—?" she began.

But he had already begun to drag her away toward the exit of the ballroom and into a hallway of parlors that were often used as passionate escapes for Vivien's guests.

He had a very different intention for whatever parlor he chose.

He slammed the first door he came to open, only to find one of the ladies in attendance down on her knees pleasuring a gentleman. The two looked up in annoyance, but then the lady continued her work with as much flourish as if no one were in the room at all.

John grumbled an apology and closed the door again. What they had seen only inflamed him further, for it made him picture *Mariah* in a similar position, giving some faceless new man pleasure with equal abandon. Some man who would take her and claim her as John had always pretended he did not wish to do.

He jerked open the next door and found the room empty. He pulled Mariah inside and slammed it behind them as she yanked her arm free and glared at him. But now that they were alone, he had a strange desire not to rail at her...but to do something far more pleasurable. Something resembling what had been happening in the room next door.

"What the hell is wrong with you?" Mariah asked as she rubbed her arm.

John blinked, his erotic fantasies fading to the background as he stared at her. "You cannot be serious. What the hell is wrong with *me*? What the hell is wrong with *you*?"

Mariah paced away from John to stand at the fire, hoping to regain some control over her racing heart and ragged breathing. She hadn't even known he was in attendance tonight, though she should have guessed. John Rycroft was well-known for his love of women and passion. Where better to find both than at one of Vivien's fetes?

"And to think," she said as she turned toward him, hoping she was hiding her strong reaction to him. "I was actually happy to see you when you came across the room."

Her words made the flashing emotion in his dark brown eyes fade and he shifted. "You were?"

She nodded. "Oh yes. Foolish as it now sounds, a friendly face was so welcome to me in this odd and untenable situation. Clearly I was mistaken to see you as an oasis to confusion and humiliation when you would grab me…accost me…drag me off like some kind of barbarian staking his claim."

The last sentence gave her a sudden image of John taking her out in an open field, spread out over fur rugs, but she shook it away.

John shifted and his face was taut with tension. "God damn it, Mariah, this is madness and I shall not be distracted from that fact. What the hell are you doing here?"

She hesitated. She had been uncertain of his emotions when he grabbed her, but now she could see…he was *angry*. Over the years she had known John, she had seen many moods from him. Yes, he was often pensive, distracted when he thought no one was observing him.

But she had never seen him angry.

She drew back. "I—" she began, unable to put any strength in her tone in the face of his unexpected wrath.

He shook his head. "I have been told you are seeking a new protector. Tell me that rumor isn't true."

Mariah flinched and her first reaction was to run from that fact, from this thing she did not wish to do. But she couldn't do that, no matter how much she desired that escape. There was one powerful reason why she couldn't bury herself in mourning and cloister herself away from leering eyes.

She drew a deep breath and calmed herself. "Why wouldn't that be true?" she asked when she found her voice again.

John's eyes widened. "Because Heathcote has only been dead a few weeks!"

Once again, Mariah couldn't help but turn her face away from those harsh words and the pain they caused. She pursed her lips and forced herself to think about the facts of her situation rather than the fact of Owen's loss.

"Yes," she said softly. "Indeed, some might call me cold to search for a new relationship while Owen is hardly in the grave. But it isn't as straightforward as you seem to think. There are circumstances at play here that you don't fully understand."

For a moment John's face, which was normally so difficult to read, revealed a flash of dismay. A moment of guilt. But no surprise. No question as to what she could be talking about.

And in that moment, Mariah stared in pure horror as the truth became clear.

"Or perhaps you understand them after all," she whispered. He shifted and his guilty expression intensified.

"I don't know what you could mean, Mariah," he said, but his voice revealed the lie in those words.

She blinked and stepped toward him, almost against her will. "Y-You knew?"

He stepped back an equal distance. "You are being foolish. Knew what?" he asked, but the rough rasp that continued in his voice, the way he turned his gaze from her told her more than his questioning denial.

"You *knew*," she repeated without clarifying.

Her entire body began to shake as she stared at John. Here was a man who had been best friends with her lover for as long as they had been old enough to walk. John had been through thick and thin with Owen. She knew they had shared secrets and even women before Owen took her as a lover.

They had been as close as two men could be.

But Mariah had also thought John counted *her* as a friend. That he cared for her on some level that was separate from his feelings for Owen. She had never believed he would allow her to be harmed if he could prevent that from happening. But that belief was apparently as untrue as Owen's promises. Both men had played her for a fool. And John was the only one she could confront.

"I really don't know what you're going on about, Mariah," John said in a harsh whisper. "Truly."

"Bollocks," she snapped as she charged on him, much as he had charged on her in the ballroom. "You *knew* that Owen was leaving me destitute, didn't you?"

"Mariah—" he began, and yet still he could not look at her.

"Didn't you?" she repeated, far louder. "Please do not treat me like an idiot now. Don't lie to me."

He hesitated, which was answer enough. Then he nodded. "Yes. Yes, I knew."

Mariah didn't think, she only reacted. "You bastard." Then she swung her hand for a slap.

CHAPTER 3

John saw Mariah's palm rounding toward his face in slow-motioned disbelief. He had never pictured her to be inspired to violence. Especially by him!

He reacted just as he would have in an underground fight. He reached up and caught Mariah's hand midair, then spun her around, trapping her in the crossing of her own arms. He pulled her back against his chest so that she could no longer use her body as a weapon.

She struggled against him, her backside gyrating over his crotch as she attempted to pull away. Her motions mimicked far more pleasurable acts. Ones best performed naked. He could hardly stifle a groan of pleasure.

Her body was still a weapon. Just not that kind she had attempted to make it a moment before.

"Let me go," she squealed as she continued to squirm and wriggle in his arms. "You son of a bitch, release me at once!"

He could hear her tears in her voice and the sound cut him as deeply as a knife to the heart. His desire to fuck vanished, replaced by another troubling need to help her. He squeezed his eyes shut as he tried to block out that strange instinct to comfort, but it was stronger than he was, at least in this moment.

He spun her around so he could look at her as they spoke. Also so that her finely curved backside would stop tormenting his rapidly hardening cock.

"Mariah, stop," he ordered in as firm a tone as he could manage. "Stop."

She squirmed a little more, but slowly the movements ceased and she simply stared up at him, eyes wide and filled with tears that she blinked to keep from shedding.

"How could you not tell me?" she whispered. "You were supposed to be my friend."

He jolted. "Is that what you think?" he asked, flattening his palm against her back and molding her against him even closer.

She stared up at him, eyes wide in the firelight, breath short. Everything between them shifted in that moment. She recognized that he wanted her. Better yet, he saw no resistance to that in her trembling body or wide-eyed stare. In fact, he saw a faint flicker of her own desire mirrored in there. Unexpected and glorious.

He couldn't help it. He lowered his mouth to hers and kissed her.

John had dreamed of kissing Mariah for as long as he'd known her. Her mouth was made for the act, with its full lips and pert tilt. That and...*other* activities they had already witnessed in the next room a moment ago. The thought had him groaning against her lips, and to his surprise, she took advantage of his parted mouth. She drove her tongue between his lips and tasted him.

But whatever control she exerted in that moment was lost as he immediately went wild. He dragged his hand into her hair, tilting her head for greater access and lifted her ass with the other, grinding her against his erection so she would know what he wanted. What he was.

She yanked away to stare at him, panting with the same desire and confusion that was painted all over her face.

"We were many things while Owen was alive," he murmured.

"But I was *never* your friend, Mariah. You can feel that now, can't you?"

He accentuated the statement by circling his hips against hers. She let out a strangled moan as his hard cock moved against her soft thighs.

There was no going back. John wasn't certain when he'd realized that, but it was so true now. He was going to do what he'd dreamed of doing for years. He was going to fuck her. And since it was an act unlikely to be repeated, he was going to do it for as long and as hard and as memorably as possible.

He backed her up until they reached the settee and pushed her back so that she sprawled across the cushions. She stared up at him, still wide-eyed.

"Tell me no," he ordered her as he stripped his jacket from his shoulders and tossed it aside. He went to work on his cravat. "Tell me to stop. That we're *friends*, Mariah. Tell me that."

She did no such thing. Instead, she remained silent as she watched him unbutton the first few buttons of his crisp linen shirt and then tug it over his head to reveal his bare chest and stomach.

Mariah sat up straighter to stare as anger was replaced with a far more complicated set of feelings. First, there was the attraction to the concept of relief. Since Owen's death, her life had been a cacophony of pain and tension. The idea of releasing some of it, here, tonight, with a lover was wildly attractive.

And then there was the second emotion—desire she had been stifling and crushing and denying for as long as she had known John. Oh yes, she could admit she had imagined what he looked like naked. In fact, she had even done so once or twice even while she lay in Owen's arms, though she banished those traitorous thoughts instantly each time.

Now the reality was far more desirable than any vague fantasy.

John was leanly muscled, with strong shoulders and an equally powerful chest that was peppered with a thin line of hair which dissipated into his trousers. Trousers that now strained with the hard, heavy erection she had felt probing her when they kissed. Even now her mouth watered at the thought of it.

He stared at her. "Speechless?"

She looked up. He was challenging her. But she was no simpering miss. She arched a brow.

"No, I can simply think of better things to do with my mouth," she purred.

She reached out to unfasten his trousers and within a few seconds, they were around his ankles and his erection was free to curl against his belly.

Despite her chosen life, Mariah had little experience with cocks. She had seen Owen's, of course. She'd had a lover before him, for a brief few months, who had been far less impressive. And then she caught a glimpse every once in a while of a man at one of these kinds of parties, like the one in the chamber next door, who had probably already spent all over his lover's ample breasts and was now back inside the party like nothing had happened.

But she had to stare at John's cock to truly enjoy it. He was thick and long, the length dark with arousal and hard as steel. She couldn't help it, not when presented with such a treat. She reached out to grasp him and pulled him closer as she shifted to her knees on the settee.

Her mouth came around him and she shivered with the intimacy of taking him into her body. He tasted salty sweet and filled her mouth with satin steel that felt like heaven.

As did his reaction. She had always seen John as a rather reserved person. Yes, he was quick to joke or laugh, but he rarely gave anyone a glimpse into his real character. He held himself away from others, using his effusiveness as a cloak, rather than an open door.

But his reaction in that moment was real. He dipped his head back over his shoulders and let out a long, low moan of pleasure that she would wager was far more emotional than he would have liked it to be. He began to thrust into her mouth, driving himself deeper and deeper into her throat. She gripped the base of his shaft harder and sucked, swirling her tongue, tasting every inch and reveling in the power she now wielded over him.

Power he seemed loath to give up, no matter how good it felt. He growled out a curse and popped himself away from her mouth. She stared for a moment at the glistening result of her handiwork, but had little time to take satisfaction in herself because he reached behind her legs and pulled her from her knees so that she dropped onto her backside on the couch. He dragged her forward on the settee and shoved her dress up and around her waist to reveal her naked body beneath.

"Trust courtesans to make this easy," he muttered.

She smiled. "*Any* woman wearing such a form-fitting dress would be naked beneath, trust me."

He dropped down before her and positioned himself before her sex. "At this point, I don't care about any other woman, Mariah."

He didn't give her a chance to respond. Instead, he gently spread her sex open and buried his mouth amongst the folds. Mariah jolted with the sensation, her back arching as he pressed the flat of his tongue along her opening again and again and again.

He was talented with his mouth, and she supposed after so many satisfied lovers, he would be. He found every sensitive fold, nipping and sucking at her flesh like she was a stream and he a thirsty man.

She relaxed back against the settee and shut her eyes, reveling in the pleasure she hadn't felt for weeks. Pleasure he doubled, tripled, when he sucked her clitoris between his lips and glided two thick fingers into her sheath.

"Oh God," she gurgled, lifting her hips to meet the strokes of his tongue and the rhythm of his fingers deep within her.

He curled the digits with each thrust, stimulating so much of her body that every heartbeat, every nerve ending, seemed to be focused on her sex. She writhed out of control as pleasure built and built and finally crested in a magnificent explosion that blurred her vision and made her scream out in the quiet room.

Shudders continued to rock her, even as he slipped his fingers from her slick sheath and gave one last lick to her spasming clit. She couldn't help the moan of displeasure as he parted from her body.

But he didn't leave her bereft for long. He draped her legs over his shoulders and positioned himself at her sex. She lifted toward the cock that pressed to her entrance.

"This is what you want?" he panted, pressing into her just half an inch.

She squeezed her eyes shut. God help her, but the answer was yes. Just a few weeks after the death of her lover, she wanted nothing more than to be taken, hard and fast, by his best friend. Despite the fact that it made her nothing better than a lightskirt trolling the streets. Despite the fact that John had offered her no future, nor had he offered a future to *any* woman in as long as she'd known him.

But those troubling facts mattered little. She wanted him inside of her. She wanted him to make her come over and over again. She wanted to feel their bodies merge just as she had always imagined they would.

"Fuck me," she said, opening her eyes to meet his gaze. "Now."

His eyes went wide on her lewd choice of words, but he obliged. He slid home in her with an impressive length of hard, heavy flesh and she felt full and dizzy with pleasure.

He cupped the back of her knees and started to thrust. His hips moved hard and fast, driving her toward pleasure, punishing her as it rose in her with a speed that was overwhelming. She had always liked sex, of course, but orgasm often took a great deal of concentration on her part. With John, there was no need for that. Her body reacted without any assistance from her mind, and pleasure mobbed her within a handful of strokes of his cock.

"John!" she cried out, grabbing for the nearest pillow. She dug her nails in and lifted her body nearly entirely off the settee as she thrashed and quivered beneath him.

He chuckled. "Very nice, but I think we can do better."

Mariah's eyes flew open and she stared at him. He withdrew from her wet body and cupped her hips. She turned over so that her back was to him and looked over her shoulder as he glided back home deep within her.

Once more he began to take her, but this time it was in long, languid strokes that seemed to go on forever. He cupped her cloth-covered breasts from behind and arched into her, their bodies moving as one as he filled her and filled her.

Mariah couldn't believe the sensations his touch inspired. She had already found powerful release twice and now he was building her toward it, *pushing* her toward it, again.

"John," she moaned as the beginnings of her orgasm rocked her. "It's too much. God, it's too much."

He laughed against her neck. "It's never too much, Mariah."

He reached out and pressed his thumb to her clitoris and she fell over the edge of release once more. But this time, she was determined to take him with her. She pressed back on his cock, writhing in tiny, seductive circles, letting him be milked by her release.

He strained against her with every thrust, grunting as his breath came short and his hold on her grew tighter. He lost control in that moment and suddenly he withdrew. With a roar, his hot seed splashed across her backside before he collapsed against her, his breath hot and sweet against her neck.

For a long time, they lay like that, then he silently moved onto his side, dragging her against him so that they fit together, her back to his front, on the narrow couch.

Mariah's dress was probably ruined, but she didn't care. She simply folded her arms around his and lay there in satisfied silence for a long time.

She couldn't believe how *good* it had felt to be with John. Actually, she could believe it. No lady had ever said anything but that he was a passionate, giving lover. The pleasure came as no surprise.

More surprising was how *right* it felt to lose herself in John's arms and body. Because of Owen, because of the circumstances, she should have felt shame or regret or a dozen other unpleasant emotions.

Instead, she felt…peaceful. Free.

She peeked over her shoulder to find John looking at her with an appraising stare. One she couldn't truly read. But it inspired a question she had no choice but to ask.

"Does this mean you are my protector now?" she asked, keeping her tone light and teasing, even though she was highly curious about his answer.

To her surprise, his answer was not in the vein of his normal witty replies. He pulled away from her, nearly putting her off the couch in his hurry to get to his feet. He stepped back and stared down at her.

"Mariah…" He shook his head and grabbed for his trousers. "We —we can't."

She pushed up on one elbow and watched him shove his fine body back into clothing with a speed and frustration more befitting a very different kind of man, one with far less confidence in everything he ever said or did. This strong reaction was definitely not what she had expected. And yet, she did not recoil.

"Well, we just did," she pointed out, as calmly as she could. "So there is that fact to refute your statement."

He stopped fiddling with his shirt and stared at her. He was so silent and so focused for so long that she had a strong urge to shift away from his gaze. To hide her sudden embarrassment.

But she didn't. She refused to be awkward or to apologize for an act that had been desired and committed by them both. She had spent far too many nights the past few weeks questioning herself, being crushed by her decisions and her beliefs about a man she had taken to her bed.

She refused to do that ever again.

"I—" he began and then shook his head. "I have loyalty to Heathcote."

She snorted out a laugh. "Ah yes, your loyalty. That would be why you took me so thoroughly in Vivien's parlor. Your deep loyalty to your dead friend."

He flinched. "Mariah—"

She got to her feet and straightened her hopelessly wrinkled gown back over her naked body. She turned to the mirror above the fireplace and began to fiddle with her mussed hair as a way to show how unaffected she was by this event. A lie, of course, but a necessary one.

"Please," she said. "Don't trouble yourself with a passel of deceit meant to comfort me. I won't beg you to do something you clearly do not wish to do. I won't beg any man. However, I *do* need to find a long-term lover, a protector, thanks to the friend you hold so much loyalty toward. If it is not to be you, then I will simply find someone else to fill that role."

She shrugged, though the dismissive action reflected none of the confusion and disappointment in her heart.

"A pity, really," she added with a small sigh. "For tonight I think we proved we could be a quite explosive combination. At least with you, there would have been pleasure. But beggars, I'm afraid, cannot be choosers."

He shook his head and his hesitation seemed almost physically painful to him. She was surprised to recognize that it stemmed from something far deeper than a mere desire to keep himself from long-term attachments with any woman. There was something more to John that she had never been privy to until now. Something far darker and more interesting.

But finally, he simply stepped toward the door, making it clear that he had no intention to share the details of that secret with her.

"I *am* sorry, Mariah," he said quietly. "Good evening."

She didn't respond, but merely watched him go. She shook her head as he disappeared down the hallway and out of her sight.

"Damn," she muttered as she turned away from the door and looked at herself in the mirror again. She looked both well-loved and utterly confused.

She did not know how long she stood there, staring at her reflection and contemplating what she had just done, but when Vivien walked through the door behind her, she pivoted like a schoolgirl caught doing something naughty.

"There you are!" Vivien said with a smile that faded when she looked around the room.

Mariah blushed at the evidence of sex all around her—crushed velvet pillows, her mussed hair and dress, the smell of sin in the air…all were evidence of her transgression.

"What happened in here?" Vivien asked with a gaze filled with concern but also wild interest.

Mariah shrugged. "Nothing of consequence, I assure you," she said. "Just a harmless little encounter that will lead to nothing."

Vivien opened her mouth to speak, but Mariah shook her head. That was all John would allow this brief encounter to be. There was no use talking it into the ground with him or her friend. She had to let it be, let it go, and go back to the matter at hand. Find a protector and move on with her life.

Even if the idea that the encounter with John was no matter of consequence was the biggest lie she'd ever told in all her years.

CHAPTER 4

John was still on her mind and Mariah could not seem to change that fact, no matter how hard she tried. Even though several days had passed, she couldn't control the erotic dreams that woke her wet and aching. She couldn't cease the intervening thoughts that forced their way into her mind while she performed the most mundane tasks. Thoughts of John's tongue, his cock and that flash of utter dismay in his stare when she said she would find a lover one way or another haunted her day and night.

She shook her head. There was no point in considering those things overly much. She and John had shared a brief exchange of passion, that was all. Their unexpected stolen moment in time was over. Now she had to put her mind to the matter at hand.

Which was why her carriage turned down the drive toward Vivien's house for the second time in a handful of days. Her friend had promised her that tonight's party would be far more intimate a gathering, which would allow Mariah to make a closer connection with a few specific men, rather than be distracted by so many.

And by John.

"No," she said through clenched teeth as the carriage stopped. "No thoughts of him. Focus. *Focus.*"

Her footman opened the carriage door and assisted her out. As she smoothed her gown, she looked up at the fine house. Vivien had been given the place outright by one of her first lovers. The next had settled her with ten thousand pounds upon their separation. The next had helped her invest that money, as well as another ten thousand he had given her himself.

With those three men, her friend had established a fine life where she did not have to worry about income. In fact, she had only taken on one protector after those and then no more. Vivien could choose to take men to her bed who she liked now, rather than men she needed for their support.

Vivien stepped into the doorway and watched Mariah move up the steps with a smile. The two women embraced and as Mariah pulled back and linked arms with her friend, she shook her head.

"I was just pondering how much I envy you for the success you have found as a mistress," she said.

Vivien laughed. "Thank you, I suppose."

Mariah did not join her laughter. "I'm quite serious. You have established a fine life for yourself. On your own terms, no less. I know not two women in our acquaintance who have managed to do so."

Vivien's laughter faded and this time she was sincere when she said, "Thank you, Mariah. But what I have done is not the impossible. It only takes a good amount of forward thinking and constant focus on a future."

Mariah nodded. That had been her problem, of course. She had thought of the future when she was with Owen, but it had been an emotional future, not a financial one. She could see now how foolish she had been. After all, at some point he would have married and had a family to fulfill his obligation to his title.

And she had a sneaking suspicion, based on what she now knew, that she might have been released from his side at that point. It was something she never would have thought about until the reading of

Owen's will, but now it stung at her, cutting her to her core. How well had she ever known the man and his heart?

She shook her head at the troublesome thought. "I was also pondering how much I admire your ability to separate your emotions from the acts of your body. I endeavor to be more like you this time. It undoubtedly makes you a happier person."

For a moment, Vivien's smile faltered a fraction and a brief sadness filled her eyes. But then it was gone, leaving Mariah uncertain if she had truly seen it at all.

"You would think it would make a person happier, wouldn't you?" her friend said.

She motioned to her parlor as they entered. A handful of ladies and gentlemen were in attendance, but no more than ten of each. As Mariah and Vivien entered, all eyes briefly turned to them.

"Our final party member has arrived, Miss Mariah Desmond," Vivien announced to the group at large. "I welcome you all."

There was a murmur of thanks and then the small group returned to their conversations. Mariah gazed around the room. There were several unattached men, at least when it came to mistresses, in the room. In fact, she had exchanged words with a few of them at the last party she had attended here.

Right before she was hauled away by John. She frowned. What they must think of her!

"Do you believe any of them will judge me because of what happened at your last party?" Mariah whispered.

"You mean when John dragged you away so publicly? Not to mention that you were forced to leave thanks to your dress being ruined?" Vivien asked.

When Mariah nodded, Vivien smiled.

"Oh yes. But I would think their judgments will be positive, indeed. The men in our circles all envy John. The women he beds are seen as trophies, for it is well known he only takes the best."

Mariah swallowed hard. That sentence only made her imagine

John now bedding some other nameless, faceless person and not even thinking of her at all.

"Well, at least *something* positive can come of that, then," she said with a bitter smile.

Vivien stared at her. "Aside from what you have described to me as an encounter of highly intense passion."

Mariah shrugged. "Yes, it was that. But then he tossed me aside."

Vivien's brow wrinkled. "You could not expect more. We all know his temperament. Once again, I caution you not to ask for more than a man can give in any relationship you develop. That will only lead to heartache, of which you have already suffered enough, I think."

Mariah nodded. Her friend was correct. It was time to become ruthless in her search and stop involving emotion of any kind.

"All right, then," she said with renewed resolve. "Tell me which of these men would make the most advantageous match for me as a lover?"

Vivien's brow arched. "As a lover or a protector?"

Mariah hesitated and then nodded. She took Vivien's meaning perfectly.

"Protector," she corrected.

Her friend's quick nod and grin rewarded her. "In that case, I *must* reintroduce you to Viscount Rossington."

She took Mariah's hand and began to lead her toward a middle-aged man standing at the fireplace. Her heart sank. He was not unattractive by any means, but certainly he was not the kind of man Mariah would choose for a lover if she had every option in the world.

Except she didn't. Owen had ensured that. So she smiled as Vivien stopped before the viscount.

"My lord, I'm not certain if you have ever met Miss Desmond."

Mariah forced a dazzling smile, told herself to be mercenary, and desperately tried to forget the feel of John's hands on her as she fell into conversation.

~

John sprawled across his bed...alone. He didn't think he'd spent a night alone in two years, and now it had been three. Three since he had plunged his cock deep within Mariah's trembling pussy and made her scream his name. Somehow the idea of any other woman now seemed stale and troublesome.

He stared at the canopy above his bed. Normally, he took a woman and never thought of her again. It wasn't that he didn't repeat pleasure. Certainly there had been lovers he revisited from time to time. But never twice in a row.

And yet all he wanted was Mariah. He wanted to spread her naked on his bed. He wanted to take her in a bath scented by roses. He wanted to fill her while they watched others make love at one of Vivien's most special and secret parties.

He groaned as his cock sprang to attention at his erotic thoughts. Fuck, but the woman was like a drug. One he had avoided for years. But now that he'd had that little taste...he wanted more.

He grabbed his cock and stroked as he pictured Mariah, her red hair down around her shoulders, leaning over him with a knowing smile. Owen had occasionally talked about her. How she had certain very sensitive places on her body. Her breasts, for example, which John had not uncovered during their encounter. He had cupped them, though, and could picture them in his mind. How he would suck them, bite them, tease them as she writhed beneath him, moaning and begging for more.

He stroked harder and grunted as pleasure built deep in his loins, increased with every stroke and every thought of her.

Taking her had been as fantastic as he had always imagined, but in his excitement he had done it too quickly. He could well imagine how incredible it would be to drag that pleasure out. To use all the techniques he knew to make love to her for hours at a time, until she was weak from orgasm after orgasm, until she ached from release and trembled like a virgin on her wedding night.

Only then would he come. Only then would he find his own pleasure.

His cock spurted and splashed seed across his stomach and bed sheets and John flopped backward against the pillows with a groan of relief.

He lay there for a long moment, enjoying the blessed emptiness of his mind. It didn't last. Almost immediately, his thoughts returned to Mariah.

Right now she was probably out seeking a new lover. And once she found one, she would be faithful to him. Any chance John had to press himself inside of her, to make her scream and cry out and declare him her best lover, was over.

And he longed to have her one last time before that happened.

He covered himself and rang for his valet. Thomason entered the room almost at once and nodded, unfazed by John being abed so late in the afternoon or by his general state of undress.

"Yes, sir?" he asked.

John sat up. "Did you do as I asked and ascertain the schedule of Miss Desmond?"

Again the valet did not appear surprised by this request, nor had he when John made it a few days before. "I did, sir. Miss Desmond is currently at an afternoon gathering at the home of Miss Manning."

John frowned. Just as he had expected, she was back out on the prowl.

"Go to my wardrobe," he ordered the servant as he threw back the covers. "I will be joining their party and I must make haste."

Mariah was doing her best to keep a seductive smile on her face and a flirtatious manner to her speech, but it seemed to be a losing battle. Certainly the task was far more difficult than Vivien made it look. She would really have to talk to her friend about how she did it.

But first, she would need to survive this gathering. After a chat with Viscount Rossington, she had then talked with Lord Felix, a very rich second son of a duke or some such thing. And now she had moved on to the Earl of Bosforth. At least he was younger than the others, but his wit left a great deal to be desired. However, Vivien had pointed out that he had settled his last two mistresses very well, which meant she was a fool not to examine him closely as a prospect.

All of the men were clearly examining her with equal zeal. Her bosom had been the recipient of several long conversations. It never replied, but she did her best to fill the gaps.

Was this *truly* how women found men for this position? Because it was exhausting and more than a little disheartening.

She glanced over her current companion's shoulder into the center of the room in hopes she could catch Vivien's eye and perhaps maneuver herself into a moment away from leering eyes. Instead, she saw Viscount Rossington slipping through the crowd, his dark gaze fixed upon her.

She sighed. He was the one who insisted on speaking to her breasts. But she managed not to scowl as he inserted himself into her conversation with the earl.

"I'm sorry, my lord," he said. "But do you think I might steal Miss Desmond away for a stroll on the veranda?"

The earl pursed his lips but nodded. "Miss Desmond, I hope we will have a chance to speak again before the afternoon is over."

Mariah smiled and took the viscount's arm. She didn't really want to go with him, but a breath of air on the veranda sounded delicious. At least she could enjoy the scenery while they talked.

The viscount held the door for her and she was allowed to release his arm as she stepped outside. She took full advantage and walked to the terrace wall where she looked out over Vivien's beautiful gardens.

Few knew it, but her friend tended several of the little plants herself, nursing them from baby seeds all the way to mature bushes with blooming roses or other fragrant flowers. Of course she had a fleet of gardeners to do the same, but she always told Mariah that she wanted something for herself. Mariah knew the feeling.

"Miss Desmond, I must say that although I am surprised to find you available for a new protector already, I *am* pleased," Lord Rossington said.

Mariah forced her attention back to him. His direct statement certainly made him more interesting. His face was rounded, soft and with a few fine lines around his mouth and eyes. There was gray at his temples, and not just a smattering. But he was not entirely unattractive. He had nice eyes. Except when they were roaming southward…yet again.

She gritted her teeth.

"I hope no one will judge me too harshly on returning to the field so soon after Owen's death," she said softly. "His loss pains me greatly, of course."

He nodded. "It was a great shock to all of Society, I assure you. But I doubt anyone would think much of you coming back to the world. After all, it wasn't as if you were his wife. You must look out for yourself, musn't you? To the satisfaction of a great many men, I assure you."

Mariah supposed he meant that comment as a compliment, but his words cut. They were a reminder that mistresses were seen as a commodity. A servant for the bedroom. No one had questioned it when Owen's housemaids sought new positions immediately. Why would they blink at her doing the same? Her heart, her feelings, her memories meant little to anyone.

She was, in some ways, seen only as the body Lord Rossington couldn't stop staring at.

"But we should not speak of such things," he continued and stepped closer. She could feel his body heat now. Smell the faint remnants of whatever scent his valet sprinkled on his clothing.

"What should we speak of?" she squeaked, hoping she managed to sound flirtatious.

He smiled, so she must have succeeded. "Perhaps we should not speak at all."

He cupped her chin and tilted her face up. His mouth came down and then his lips were on hers. Mariah squeezed her eyes shut and did not pull away, even though a deep part of her wanted to refuse the kiss. This was what and who she was, there was to be no simpering about it.

Except, as Lord Rossington parted his lips over hers and pushed his tongue past her lips, Mariah felt nothing. There was no disgust, thankfully, but no desire, either. There was not even the pleasant tingle associated with the act of kissing this man. She felt no attraction to him whatsoever.

He continued to kiss her and even dragged her closer, but her mind raced. How would she make love to him if she felt nothing?

She couldn't.

With a gentle hand on his chest, she pushed away and took a step back.

"I-I'm sorry," she began. "But I cannot do this."

He stared at her and suddenly those dark eyes grew far less kind. He sneered as he looked her up and down, no longer lustfully, but disdainfully.

"What do you mean you cannot do this?" he repeated. "*This* is what you do."

She drew a short breath. There was no use becoming angry or upset by his demeanor. It was best to stay calm.

"My lord," she began, hoping deference to his place would smooth the situation. "You are correct that a woman like me is in a certain...position. But I'm afraid I must feel some kind of connection to a gentleman before I can develop a relationship."

He arched a brow and his disdain seemed to deepen. He looked at her like she was trash. "A woman like *you* doesn't get to say no."

With that, he grabbed her arm and yanked her against him a second time. His mouth ground on hers again, this time punishing and cruel. Her arm hurt where he manhandled her and her mouth stung from the hardness of his kiss. Fear rose up in her, but she was soothed by the knowledge that just a few steps away were people who would come to her aid. Vivien would likely come looking for her in a moment.

And yet he continued to kiss her as punishment, even as she struggled for escape.

"My lord," she insisted against his mouth. "Please!"

She said nothing more because suddenly her companion was torn away from her side. She staggered backward, nearly ending up on her ass as she watched John grab the man and throw him aside like he was made of paper.

Lord Rossington fell to his side on the hard veranda floor, but was up quickly, especially for a man of his years.

"And just what is this, Rycroft?" he barked.

John moved toward him in one long step and Rossington retreated just as quickly. Mariah could scarcely do anything but stare as John leaned over her attacker.

"Touch her again and I rip your head off," John growled. And it was truly a growl, like an animal being held just at bay by an unseen master.

He turned toward her now, and the anger in his stare didn't diminish even as he moved toward her.

"Are you hurt?" he bit past thin lips.

She opened her mouth to speak but could find no words, so instead merely shook her head.

"Not yet," John muttered and shot Rossington another glare. The other man was dusting himself off.

"Please, Rycroft," the viscount said with a dismissive glare. "She's nothing, certainly not worth making an enemy in *me*."

Mariah held her breath. The viscount was right in some ways. He had a title and position in the world. And John, while rich and the son of a second son, might not want to cross him. Certainly a great many men would throw over a no one of a girl like her long before they treated Rossington with disregard.

But John didn't even hesitate. He looked Rossington up and down in much the same way Rossington had looked at her—with pure contempt dripping from him.

"*You* are a worm of a man. You have what…five thousand a year to your name and an estate that your poor management is running into the ground? I would wager that in ten years, you'll be lucky to drag in thirty-five hundred per annum."

Mariah stared at the viscount, who shifted under John's words. His face darkened and she knew what John said was true to its core.

But he wasn't finished. He continued, "You should more fear losing my regard than trying to intimidate me with the loss of yours. I should scarcely notice it if it were gone."

He reached out and took Mariah's elbow, though there was no violence to his touch. None of the anger that seemed to make his eyes glow.

"Come, we're leaving," he ordered and marched her not to the terrace door leading back to the parlor with the others but to another empty parlor.

She hesitated as he dragged her inside.

"What are you doing?" she asked.

He hesitated. "Taking you home," he finally admitted and she caught her breath in surprise and a desire that seemed to flame up from nowhere.

"I thought you were finished with me," she said softly.

He stared at her for a long moment. "Apparently not."

CHAPTER 5

Mariah had been curiously quiet on the drive through the busy city streets to his London townhome. He had expected her to resist, argue, perhaps even try to bolt...a dozen things except what she was doing—sitting across from him in the carriage, arms folded and face utterly unreadable. Her stare was only made more uncomfortable by her absolute silence. He had no idea what she thought about his sudden intrusion into Vivien's party, his sweeping her away or his forcefulness when it came to Lord Rossington.

His blood boiled at just the thought of the man. When he stepped onto the terrace to find Mariah fighting to get free from the other man's unwanted embrace, something in him had snapped, as it hadn't since...well, for a great many years. He could have killed the viscount in that moment. Only a great deal of restraint and common sense kept him from doing so. Being transported was not a pleasant future and he had no interest in it happening.

His footman opened the door to the carriage and Mariah took the hand he offered before John could exit the rig. She swept up the stairs as if she owned the place and past his gaping butler, Swanson.

She had been to John's home with Owen many a time and moved into a parlor without asking his leave.

Despite the situation, John couldn't help but smile at her boldness and he lifted a hand to show Swanson that this odd turn of events was acceptable to him.

"No interruptions," he said to the man. "Thank you."

He shut the door firmly behind him and turned to speak to Mariah. Instead, she folded her arms and began the conversation herself.

"John, you do vex me," she said.

John blinked. "I—I beg your pardon?"

She shook her head and paced to the sideboard where she poured herself a scotch and took a sip. She grimaced at the strength of the liquor and continued.

"While I do appreciate the sentiment behind your little rescue this afternoon, your heavy-handedness cannot be borne."

John blinked. "I believe it was more than a 'little rescue'. That man had intentions—"

She tilted her head. "Indeed, he did. And they were far less than honorable. I had already told the viscount no and he did not seem to understand that word, especially coming from a person who he would deem...actually *did* deem...a whore."

She said the words so very calmly, but John could see from the brief flash in her eyes how deeply those words cut her.

"Still, I do not think I was in any *true* danger," she continued. "After all, the parlor was a mere three feet away and Vivien would have come to rescue me eventually."

"*Eventually*," John repeated blankly. "How can you dismiss what was about to happen so easily? That man would have raped you had he had the chance."

She flinched and it took her a few seconds to respond. "I suppose that could have happened, yes. But my virtue was sold away years ago. What happens to my body has less effect now than it once would have."

John stared, eyes wide. "That is the worst fucking thing I have ever heard. You are *not* a whore, no matter what he said. Even if you were, no man has a right to force himself on you in such a manner. It is disgusting."

She lifted her eyebrows delicately. "I appreciate that you think highly enough of me to believe I have a right to decide what my path and who my lover should be. I hope there are more men out there like you. But honestly, John, you are the last person who should have ridden to my rescue today. You were not invited to Vivien's gathering, for one."

He pursed his lips. That was true. When he burst into the parlor, Vivien had appeared quite annoyed with him. Despite that fact, she hadn't stopped him when he'd gone racing to the veranda, nor interfered when he swept Mariah away like the Gothic hero of some ridiculous novel.

"Secondarily, and perhaps more importantly..." Mariah hesitated. "You have made it more than clear that you do not want me."

John blinked. Had those words just come from her mouth? Did she truly believe that after he had spent three days pleasuring himself to forget her, thinking of her constantly, and then racing to her side like a forlorn puppy?

"I don't want you," he repeated with a shake of his head.

He didn't think of what he did next. It was all instinct and drive that made him clench his fists and storm across the room to her. He caught her arms, drew her against him and kissed her.

She was still for a moment, but then she made a muffled groan. Her arms came up around his neck and she lifted herself against him, driving her tongue to meet his. He felt and tasted her desire. Her surrender. It was heady and sweet against his lips. He wanted so much more of it.

Without his saying so, she obliged. Her hips began to lift in a slow, steady rhythm against his and he was lost. He pushed her backward until they hit the wall next to the window.

He cupped her backside to lift her against him and she moaned as their eyes met. He smiled and began to slowly shift his weight against her in slow, sensual circles. She shivered and he could tell he was hitting her in just the right spot to make her wet with wanting, a theory he was very excited to test. But not yet.

Instead, he continued holding her against him with one hand and with the other he found her breast. She gasped and her back arched as he cupped her. He hadn't stripped her of her gown the last time they made love. Everything had been so heated and fast in Vivien's parlor that he wouldn't have been able to wait.

Now he could and he wanted to see her naked. He wanted to feel the full softness of her body pressed to his and watch the way her skin flushed and her nipples pebbled when he worked her in this way and that.

He released her and swiftly turned her to face the wall. She gasped, but lifted her backside against him with another moan of pleasure as her hands fisted and flexed against his wallpaper. He leaned forward to press a kiss to the back of her neck, suckling her tender flesh as he flicked open the buttons of her gown.

He pushed the gown forward and she gave him enough space that he was able to strip it to her waist, followed swiftly by the sheer chemise she wore beneath. Then he turned her back toward him and stared to his heart's delight.

Mariah's dark auburn hair was complemented perfectly by her pale skin. Her breasts were the ideal size to fill his hands and their peaks were topped with pink nipples that were currently swollen and hard with desire.

He leaned forward and sucked one into his mouth. Mariah's hands slid into his hair and she held him steady as she gasped and moaned in time to his tongue. He swirled it around the bud, laving and sucking, nipping and gently scraping his teeth over the peak.

She mumbled an indiscernible sound of pleasure and shimmied her hips out of the remainder of her gown so that she stood utterly naked before him.

He was undone. His cock throbbed against his trousers and his whole body was poised, ready to explode.

"Some day the time will come when I will take my time with you," he promised. "I'm certain at some point this madness that steals my control will cease."

~

Mariah's lips parted in surprise at his statement. John was known for his restraint with lovers—how could it be that *she* stole that from him? She might have asked, but at that moment John stripped his shirt over his head and shucked his boots and trousers off. She could scarcely breathe, let alone speak, as she stared at him.

They were naked together. She never would have dreamed that would ever happen. But here they were. He stepped forward and dragged her against him. His mouth came to hers again, rough and demanding, but utterly and sinfully pleasurable. She lost herself when he tasted her, sucking her tongue like he had laved her tingling nipple.

He lifted her and she wrapped her legs around his hips without any urging. For a brief moment, time was suspended there. She pressed against the wall, his cock poised and hard at her entrance, she drew back and stared at him, their eyes locked.

And then time moved again and he thrust deep within her. She was so wet and ready that he encountered no resistance. Pleasure tore at her as he breached her for the second time in just a few days. Pleasure just as intense and overwhelming as it had been the first time they were in this position.

He cupped her tightly and she clung to his shoulders until her nails bit into his skin as he began to thrust. Almost immediately the grind of his pelvis against her clitoris had pressure and pleasure burning in her. She gasped, clinging to him as her hips jerked out of control.

The orgasm hit like a storm out of nowhere. It was violent and powerful, stealing her breath, her voice, her ability to control her body. John thrust through it, giving her no mercy as she called out his name again and again.

Just when she thought it was over, just when her body's trembling subsided a fraction, he strained, his thrusts becoming erratic, and with a growl, his cock pumped within her. The feel of him bursting inside of her blew her over the precipice she was so delicately balanced upon and she came a second time, this time a smaller, gentler version of her earlier explosive burst.

For a long time, they leaned against the wall, foreheads pressed together, breathing matched. They were one body, bound by the passion they'd shared. Mariah didn't think she'd felt so close to a lover before.

As if he sensed those deeper thoughts, John kissed her cheek with such gentleness that it brought tears to her eyes and withdrew from her.

The loss of their intertwined bodies left Mariah bereft, but she said nothing and instead began to look around for her long ago discarded gown. John dressed himself swiftly, but her dress and underthings were more complicated. She stepped into the gown and then looked at him from the corner of her eye.

"Er, could you?" she asked, suddenly shy and awkward around a man she had not only called friend for years, but who had just soundly fucked her against a parlor wall.

"Of course," he said and turned her so her back was to him.

Mariah was glad not to face him. He was so disconcerting to her now. They had been friends, except not. They were now lovers... except not. She never knew what to expect from him when once he had been such a steadfast part of her life.

"Have I proven you wrong?" he asked softly as he fastened the last button.

"Wrong?" she repeated, her brain too foggy from release to fathom what he could mean.

He chuckled and the deep sound reverberated through her sensitive body. "You said I didn't want you. Have I proven you wrong?"

She turned to look at him. "I—I suppose it is evident you *do* want me after all," she conceded with a shrug. "But you do not want to be my protector."

His smile fell and he turned to look out the window. He was quiet for a long moment, then he muttered, "I'm no one's protector, trust me, Mariah."

Once again, Mariah sensed his anger. That was twice in just a handful of days, when she had never felt such strong emotion from him before.

She longed to know why this topic inspired such an intense reaction, but was in no position to ask him. They were not in a relationship, despite this second surrender to desire. Even if they were, that kind of intimacy could only lead to heartache. She refused to develop feelings for any man she took to her bed again.

She shrugged off her desire to know more and said, "Then what *do* you want, John? Because I cannot for the life of me fathom your secret plans."

He sat down on the settee and rubbed his eyes. "You and I have known each other for a great many years, Mariah," he said. "I will be as honest with you as I am able, for I feel you deserve that, especially after Owen's deceptive actions."

Mariah flinched at the reminder, but then nodded. "Thank you. I appreciate the respect honesty implies more than you know."

"Please sit." He motioned to the chair near him.

She took it and watched as he rang for tea.

It was amazing. They had just wrapped themselves around each other, coupled with wild, animal abandon and now the servants brought in a service as if nothing had happened. As if this were a normal little meeting between friends.

The servants left and John motioned for her to pour. She did so, sweetening his tea just as she remembered he liked it. As he took a sip, he smiled.

"Mariah, I want to admit to you that I have desired you greatly," he said as he set his cup down.

Mariah had just taken a sip of her own tea and began to choke on the contents with surprise at his admission. Once she had regained her breath, she stared at him.

"I beg your pardon?"

He nodded. "From the first moment I saw you, I wanted you. It was the night of the Nethercourt gathering three years ago. You wore a green gown and your eyes seemed to be alive with color. You entered the room and I had to have you… I would have had you, except that Owen told me you were his new mistress."

Mariah blinked in increasing disbelief at the detail John could recount of the night of their first meeting. "I—I had no idea of your feelings."

"Of course not." John frowned. "I made certain you did not, nor did Owen. I would not have betrayed him in such a manner. But my desire for you never decreased. Although I suppose that fact is rather clear since I have taken you not once, but twice in recent days. And without much finesse either time, for which I apologize."

Mariah set her cup away and leaned back in the chair to stare at him. "You act as though I received no pleasure from those encounters. I assure you, I did. A great deal, both times."

He smiled, almost in relief. "Good. I would hate to think I have left a poor impression."

Even though she wanted to smile at his teasing, she hesitated. They could flirt with each other about the pleasure of their coupling all day, but there was a deeper topic to be addressed and she shifted back to it.

"I admit, while there was always an attraction between us, I had no idea you truly desired me. Until you…claimed me at Vivien's party last week."

"And do you desire me, as well?" he pressed.

She cocked her head. "You must be in jest asking that question. Clearly, I want you. In fact, there is no other—"

She stopped. Was it wise to tell this man that thus far he was the *only* one she desired? That she could picture herself in no other man's bed?

Probably not.

His eyes widened at her truncated statement, but he did not press her further.

"Good," he said slowly. "At least this madness affects us both."

She nodded. He had said madness twice and that was as good a way to put these feelings as any. It certainly seemed like madness when he touched her and she lost control like some untried virgin who had only just discovered pleasure and wanted to explore it in every way possible. When it was only the fact that Owen was gone, a fact that hurt them both so desperately, that gave them the power to pursue their desire.

"But again, I ask you what to do about it?" she pressed as she got to her feet and paced the room restlessly. "We want each other, we have each admitted as much, but that does not solve my problem, nor does it make you want to take the role of protector for me."

He nodded. "I understand. But since you do not yet have a protector...and since my desire for you continues despite my vow never to have the same woman two times in a row...perhaps what we should share is an affair."

Mariah blinked. "An...affair?" she repeated slowly.

"Yes. Something that is just for us, just for you."

He pushed to his feet and moved a step toward her. There was something almost desperate in his eyes as he stared at her. Like he needed this, just as she needed it.

"Mariah, you will soon enter into a new relationship and I'm sure you will be well taken care of, but would you not like to also have a few weeks where you just experience *pleasure*? I would give that to you. If you would allow me to do so."

Mariah shivered. John had proven himself a powerful lover

already. She knew there was more waiting for her if she accepted his offer. And perhaps, in some small way, being with him would help her open the doors so that she would be *ready* for a new lover, a new protector.

"I admit, it is tempting," she said, glancing at him from the corner of her eye. "*You* are tempting, though I'm certain you know that better than anyone."

His quick flash of a grin did not dissipate her feelings on the subject, but she pressed on.

"But, John, you must understand, my current situation is quite dire. Yes, there is a small bit of money, but in six months I shall lose my home—" She stopped with a blush. "I shall lose the home Owen provided for me during our arrangement. I would very much like to be in a new situation before that happens. Before I must beg off the kindness of my friends. Before I become truly desperate. I cannot simply call off my search for a protector...even if we are sharing passion and pleasure."

For a moment, John hesitated.

"I admit, I don't like the idea that you would continue to seek out a lover even while coming to my bed," he began slowly. "But I am aware of the untenable position Owen left you in. I realize what you are facing."

Mariah bit her lip. "Yes, there is that fact. That you knew what Owen intended and did not share it with me."

He frowned and for the first time since their first meeting, he actually looked chagrined. "I suppose I hoped he would change his mind."

"Wh-why didn't Owen make arrangements for my comfort?" she whispered. In her heart she knew why. He had not loved her, all his promises had been empty, a way to make her surrender fully, to cease her worries so that she would only focus on him. But she wanted to hear it said out loud.

"Heathcote was selfish. He had never experienced any kind of fear or loss financially, so he could not empathize with the idea of such a thing." John shrugged. "I'm certain he would have settled you well if he had left you instead of died. But he could not picture a time when he would be gone…and if he had…he was too conceited to plan for anyone else's comfort. Hell, he probably thought the world would end with him."

Mariah shook her head. The words themselves were a harsh assessment of a man she had loved. But they were accurate. Owen's sense of his own importance, his sense of his worth to others, had never been a secret. That confidence had once been an attraction. She had expected him to change his stripes, perhaps that had been to her detriment.

"I must be more careful with my next lover," she said, raising her gaze to meet his. "And choose a protector wisely, as well."

He nodded after a brief hesitation. "I would not ask you to endanger yourself for my pleasure. It would be unfair."

Mariah drew back. She hadn't expected him to understand, yet he did. "Thank you."

He looked at her evenly. "Does that mean we have come to terms?"

Mariah jolted. "Is that what we have been doing? Negotiating?" He nodded and she couldn't help but laugh. "I should have had a representative here, I think."

"Trust me, I have your best interest at heart." He smiled. "Or at least your best interest is paramount to *some* part of my body."

She smiled. Here she was, in an untenable position, and yet John somehow made light of it. Made her laugh when she hadn't even felt like smiling for weeks. That, at least, was worth pursuing.

"Then I suppose we *have* come to terms," she said and stepped forward to take his hand. "I must say, I most look forward to fulfilling them."

He grinned as he looked down at her. "As do I."

She shook her head and lifted his hand to her breast, which now ached with the desire to be touched, yet again, by him. She had never felt such strong need before. Even with Owen, they made love and she was satiated. Not that they didn't do the same over and over some nights, but she had never been driven by need after the first encounter, only a desire to please Owen.

This was different.

"I have never had an affair to please...and pleasure...myself," she said, trying to focus as John began to gently massage and pluck her breast with those talented fingers of his.

"No?" he asked, his gaze coming up to hers.

She shook her head. "No."

"Then we must be very certain that you are able to receive whatever you would like, whenever you would like it. As often as you would like it."

His words were teasing, but his tone and his expression were most definitely not. He never broke his stare from hers, nor did he stop touching her with those amazing hands that seemed to naturally find every spot on her body that ached.

"I am much looking forward to it."

She leaned toward him, ready to accept his kiss and give over her body to his care, once again, when there was a knock at the door. Both of them jolted, as if surprised that there were even other people still in the world around them.

John stepped back and frowned. "Yes?"

The door opened and Swanson, John's unflappable butler, stood in the entryway. "I'm sorry, sir, I know you said no interruptions, but the investors have arrived for the early supper you arranged last week."

John squeezed his eyes shut. "Yes," he grumbled. "Damn, I had forgotten." He looked at her. "I'm sorry."

She shook her head. "John, you must run your business, of course. Perhaps we could meet again later?"

"Tonight?" John asked.

She nodded. "At my home?"

He hesitated. "I...I'm not certain I wish to share a bed you once shared with my best friend."

She flushed at the reminder."Of course. Then shall I join you here?"

"Yes. At eight." He smiled. "I shall be counting the hours."

She shot a brief look toward Swanson, who stepped into the hallway. When he was gone, she lifted on her tiptoes and drew John down for a deep kiss. It spiraled out of control almost immediately and she had to force herself to pull back.

"Until tonight," she panted.

"Yes," he growled. "Tonight."

CHAPTER 6

Mariah sipped her brandy in the warmth of Vivien's private parlor. Her friend had many public parlors, in fact she was well-known for their naughty wallpaper and settees and chairs built for two. Those chambers were all about Vivien's public persona.

But in the back of her home, up the stairs, were her *real* rooms. Her comfortable and pretty private bedroom that was separate from the opulent one she had shared, and occasionally *still* shared, with lovers.

There was also a parlor done in soft blues and grays where she could share tea and conversation with friends. Even a music room where Vivien indulged her passion for the pianoforte. It was as if her friend had two lives, lived in the same home but separate from each other in every way that was meaningful.

Few had the privilege of seeing what Mariah considered the "real" Vivien. She was proud to count herself as one of them.

The door opened and her friend swept in with a wide smile. Mariah was always taken by how pretty and sophisticated Vivien was. Mariah had never quite reached those heights as a mistress, though she continually strived to do so.

"Hello, my dear," Vivien said, pressing a kiss to each cheek as

Mariah stood up. "I'm so pleased you've come. I was wondering who I might share supper with today."

Mariah laughed. "You are never at a loss for partners."

Vivien shrugged as they took their seats and she poured her own drink. "Partners, no. Friends, well, sometimes that is a very different story."

Mariah covered her free hand briefly and the two women smiled at each other for a moment.

"But I doubt you came here to wax poetic about the value of friendship for women of our station," Vivien laughed. "I haven't seen you since John Rycroft swept you out of my little afternoon soiree. Tell me, what is happening with you?"

"I don't know," Mariah admitted reluctantly.

"How can you not know?" Vivien said with a burst of pretty laughter. "It is your life, is it not?"

Mariah shrugged. "Sometimes I do wonder if that is true. I'm glad you brought John up, for he is the reason I have returned."

"Yes, I admit I am all but bursting with curiosity at this turn in his demeanor." Vivien shook her head. "I am confused by his strange behavior when it comes to you. He has always made it a matter of pride not to form any kind of attachments, yet he seems to be very attached to you."

"You know we…" Mariah hesitated. "Well, we took advantage of your parlor the night of your ball."

Vivien laughed. "Yes, I do know that. Anyone standing in the hall knew that. He must be very wicked."

Mariah blushed. Mistress she might be, but knowing that others were fully aware of her encounters was both disconcerting and titillating.

"He is that." She laughed, but it was forced. "But the association has gone a bit beyond that, I fear. You see, I assumed that night was the end of it. He made it clear he will not, or perhaps *cannot*, be my protector. And yet today he swept in out of nowhere and rescued me from Lord Rossington."

"I wondered if Rossington had become a bit too forceful with you," Vivien said with a frown. "The viscount was furious when he returned to the party."

Mariah pursed her lips. Although she had no intentions of ever allowing Rossington near her again, it wasn't a good idea to anger a man of title and such wealth.

"Will he make things difficult for me?"

Vivien shook her head. "I smoothed his ruffled feathers. But I shall not attempt to make a match for *him* again."

Mariah sighed in relief. "Your smoothing is most appreciated. And I wouldn't match Rossington again. He is...not as kind as he appears."

A flash of anger darkened Vivien's face, but then she shook it away. "So John rescued you, took you somewhere and...?"

"Well, we made love again," she sighed. "We have entered into an affair."

Vivien clapped her hands together. "Oh, quite excellent! After these recent events, I hoped that would be so. John will make an excellent protector, especially of you. Though I do caution you, he is exactly the sort of man I believe you might develop feelings for. You have been friends a long time and clearly, you share a powerful connection. I would hate to see you hurt once more, and perhaps more deeply than you were thanks to Owen."

Mariah allowed her friend to finish before she shook her head. "I —John is not my new protector."

Vivien stared for a moment and then pushed to her feet and paced away as she muttered, "Oh dear God."

"Please don't take such a tone!" Mariah insisted. "You *know* that John is the unattainable man, by lady or by mistress. He refuses to bind himself to just one woman."

Vivien snorted a sound of perturbed frustration.

"But we want each other," Mariah continued. "Apparently desperately enough that he has suggested this affair."

Vivien spun on her. "Mariah! You must see the very large numbers of reasons to worry over this arrangement."

"I know," she began, but Vivien would not allow it.

"If Owen had settled you with enough funds that you could live comfortably off the interest, as you had believed he would, then yes, you could enter into frivolous affairs. In fact, I would encourage you to do so, as they can be quite invigorating. But he didn't."

Mariah pursed her lips. "Yes, I realize—"

Vivien lifted a hand to silence her. "You *need* a protector, and sooner rather than later. Some kind of affair will only hinder that process."

Mariah pushed to her feet. "If you will let me get a word in edgewise, I will tell you that John understands that I must continue looking for a protector."

Vivien stopped and stared at her. "John Rycroft accepts the fact that you must look for a protector during the time that he is taking you in every way his wicked mind can imagine? I cannot picture that kind of arrangement is in his nature. To share you without it being in some kind of pleasurable way."

Mariah swallowed hard at the image her friend created, but shook her head. "It is an arrangement we can both live with."

Her friend continued to keep her gaze evenly on Mariah's face. "He must like you a great deal."

Mariah barked out a laugh. "No, he wants me. And I admit, I do want him. What he has offered me is pleasure, just for me. There are no expectations or boundaries. I am not expected to only give. And that is entirely bewitching."

Vivien's brow wrinkled and for a moment there was a flash of understanding on her face. Mariah wasn't entirely certain she liked what she saw. It was something akin to...*pity*.

But then Vivien nodded. "I can understand that," she said softly. "And perhaps this will lead to something more permanent."

Mariah shook her head. "I don't understand. What do you mean?"

"Only that if anyone could change a man's mind, it would be you," Vivien said with a laugh. "Spend a few weeks immersed in pleasure with him and he might not be willing to let you go. He could be entirely under your spell."

Mariah blinked. Was that possible? Could she be the one to tame John's wild heart? And what would happen if she was *his*?

"Perhaps," she said, hesitating at the thought.

Vivien sensed that hesitation. "Or do you fear you will be under his?"

Mariah jerked her gaze to her friend. "*No*. No, that would not be wise. I cannot risk love again, correct? So I will not fall under his spell. I won't involve my feelings, nor ask him to involve his. We will share only sex. Only pleasure." She sighed. "At least I can depend on John to give me that and not pretend anything more."

"No," Vivien said softly. "John will never pretend. One way or another."

Mariah pushed to her feet and walked across the room. She stared out at the street below, where carriages bustled and couples strolled toward the park just down the street from Vivien's home. She was quiet for a long time, thinking about everything Vivien had said. Thinking of everything she and John had already done.

Slowly, she turned to find Vivien watching her, her gaze filled with concern.

"You are my best friend," Mariah began. "And you are more well-versed in these types of matters than anyone in our acquaintance. So I trust you tell me the truth. You think this is a bad idea, don't you?"

Vivien's hesitation told a story before she spoke and Mariah's heart sank.

Until that moment, she hadn't truly known how much she wanted to surrender to John with utter abandon. To throw away her obligations and fears and simply *feel* with him.

Vivien got to her feet and crossed to Mariah. She wrapped her arms around Mariah's waist and squeezed.

"There are many things to consider, yes. Many pitfalls that could lead you to heartache. But, my dearest, I look at your situation and I think that you deserve some pleasure of your own. Do I believe you should tread carefully? I do, indeed."

Mariah nodded. "I agree. And I intend to tread very carefully."

Vivien smiled and gave her another squeeze, but as her friend pulled away and motioned to the door so they could proceed to supper, Mariah couldn't help but wonder if she would be able to tread carefully with John. At the moment, she wanted to run headlong into what he offered.

And that could be the biggest mistake of her life.

John looked at the clock. It was nearly eight. But then, it had been nearly eight for at least a year because that seemed to be how long he had been watching the clock since he came into his chamber to wait for Mariah. A chamber he had shared with a great many women, and yet he had never paced about it in anticipation like this before.

There was a light rap on his door and John froze. Slowly he smoothed his jacket and called out, "Come," with as calm a tone as he could manage.

The door swung open and Mariah stood in the entryway, eyes wide, face pale as she looked around slowly.

"Good evening," he managed to croak out.

She nodded. "Good evening. I…Swanson told me to come to this room at your request."

John motioned her inside. She entered slowly and then closed the door behind her with a tiny, earth-shattering click.

"I thought about meeting with you in a parlor," he explained as he slowly crossed the room to her. "And sharing a drink and some empty conversation. But eventually I realized all that would do was prolong the time it took to get here. This chamber. Where we both want to be." He took her hands and drew her closer. "Don't we?"

"Yes," she breathed and lifted up on her tiptoes to crush her mouth to his.

Any thoughts, any charming words that John had in his mind emptied in that moment. Finally, he was going to receive what he desired. Oh, he had taken Mariah before, but that wasn't enough. Tonight he would really have her. Slowly. And he intended to take advantage of every moment they would share that wasn't rushed and desperate.

He drew back and looked down at her. Her hazel stare was almost impossibly dark with desire at the moment and focused entirely on him.

"Take off your clothes," he rasped as he stepped away.

She blinked. "You don't want to take them off?"

It was said so sweetly that the words alone could hardly be taken as a challenge, but her expression was anything but sweet. She was taunting him, daring him to do so.

He shook his head. "I will rend the dress in two if I do it. And then you will be forced to leave my home utterly naked."

Her responding laughter was throaty and made his groin ache, but then she lifted her hands to the buttons of her gown. It was a different from the one she had worn earlier in the day and had buttons along the front. He stared as she flicked each one free with just a smooth motion of her wrist and parted her gown to seductively reveal the curves of her breasts.

"If I am to take off my clothing," she said with a counterfeit pout, "I think it only fair that you remove yours. None of this only one person naked while we make love nonsense."

He swallowed. She was testing his resolve and his control with her playful, seductive teasing. And truth be told, he liked it. So many women he encountered seemed intimidated by his presence, his reputation, his money, his name, that they were coy with him. They allowed him to do all the work that led to a sexual encounter. And while he enjoyed a good seduction as much as the next man…

Well, he also very much liked Mariah's confidence and boldness.

She opened the last button of her gown and parted the fabric slightly. She gently lifted and pushed her breasts together, but did not uncover them, offering him just a tantalizing glimpse of cleavage.

"Your turn," she ordered.

He did not require a second request. Without breaking their stare, he shoved out of his jacket and tossed it away from him without bothering to see where it landed. Next he unbuttoned his shirt, carefully repeating her seductive play when she had done the same with her gown.

She grinned and then laughed at his playful teasing and his heart jumped unexpectedly at her wide, pretty smile. She so often didn't show it, instead playing the part of a seductive, erotic mistress. But dear God, it was worth everything to see her so at ease, so joyful.

He stripped his shirt off and she stopped laughing and instead just stared at him.

"John," she murmured and reached for him, closing the gap between them to press her hand against his bare chest.

He sucked his breath in through his teeth and held it as she glided her fingers down his chest, over his stomach and then let them fall away.

"You approve?" he managed to ask.

She nodded and her gaze returned to his. "Oh yes. Very much so. But I'm sure you think nothing of that. Every woman who sees you like this must coo and moan over you. You know you are beautiful, a specimen. My thinking the same couldn't be of any consequence."

John stared at her. As if he could ever rank her amongst the numerous unimportant women who had touched him over the years.

"Mariah, trust that your thoughts mean a great deal to me. They always have," he said softly.

Her eyes went wide and she stared at him for so long that he shifted at the intensity of her gaze. To lighten the mood, to break the tension, he smiled.

"Now I am half-naked, and you are still fully clothed. I thought you wished to prevent this sort of disparity from occurring. It is only fair that you remove some portion of that gown."

She blinked and the spell was broken. Her smile was wobbly, but she slowly, seductively glided her gown over her shoulders and tugged it down. She held up the fabric around her chest as she slipped her arms free from each sleeve and then dropped the dress around her waist to reveal her perfect breasts.

"Dear God," he growled, almost against his will.

"Does this mean you equally approve of me?" she pressed as she glided a finger between those breasts.

He arched a brow. "Look at how my cock strains against my breeches and tell me I do not."

She let her gaze slip southward and her eyes went wide. "My, that does look uncomfortable, Mr. Rycroft. Perhaps you should remove those before you lose consciousness from a lack of blood to the rest of your body."

He chuckled as he toed off one boot, then the other and kicked them away so that when he pulled his trousers off, he could step free of their confines. Mariah leaned forward as he snapped free the first button of his trouser fly. Then the second, and she stopped breathing. The third, and he couldn't contain his erection as it strained to escape in the space he had created.

"Would you like me to help you?" she asked, all breathless innocence.

He shook his head. "Touch me now and I shall explode. Which will completely defeat the purpose. Just one more and..." He popped the last button and slipped his cock from the confines of his trousers with a sigh of relief. Then he shucked them down and away to stand utterly naked and aroused before her.

"My God, John," she whispered, all the teasing gone from her voice. "You are amazing. No wonder every courtesan, whore and mistress is willing to present herself to you at a simple word."

He shook his head. "I couldn't give less of a thought to any of them at this moment. I am now naked, madam. And you are half-clothed. Please finish what we have started."

Mariah half-smiled and then shimmied from her gown to stand before him naked. He caught his breath. He had seen her this way before, of course, but lust had been coursing through his veins too powerfully to really take in every inch of her.

She had long, willowy lines that flowed like some artist's rendition of a woman's perfect beauty.

"My God, Mariah," he breathed. "You are everything I ever imagined you to be. More than I dreamed."

She blushed. "But this is not a dream."

She moved forward and gently wrapped her arms around his neck. She lifted up to her tiptoes and kissed him. This time there was no crushing desperation, no forceful demand to their kiss. It was slow and seductive as she tangled her tongue with his, tasting him, testing the measure of his response to this or that.

He shivered at her mastery of the kiss. He didn't think he'd ever kissed a woman who affected him so deeply with just that caress. He cupped her backside and molded her more fully to his body as the kiss deepened and spiraled further and further into a place that could only end in their bodies joined and moving together toward release.

She groaned against his mouth and lifted and crooked one long, smooth leg around his thigh. The motion opened her sex and he felt its humid heat against him, welcoming him, waiting for him.

He growled his desire out and swept her up into his arms. She expelled her breath in a surprised sigh as he carried her to the bed and laid her out against his sheets. Then he stepped back to stare at her.

Her hair had come partially down and long locks of it curled around his pillows and at her shoulders. She lounged back, utterly seductive without even trying as she stared up at him in waiting.

He lifted himself onto the bottom of the bed and crawled up toward her, nuzzling her calf, her knee, then her inner thigh. Each time the slightly rough texture of his cheek caressed her, she let out a quiet moan of pleasure. Dear God, but she was responsive. And none of it was forced or falsified as so many courtesans did. Mariah pretended nothing. Not in her life and not in her lover's bed.

That fact was as bewitching as her eyes.

He parted her legs farther and opened her sex. It glistened with readiness, pink and wet. She had trimmed the hair around it, so it was almost bare but for a thin line of red curls. He stroked a finger along the slit and she arched her back with a guttural grunt.

"So tender," he teased. "Good enough to eat."

She opened her eyes, which she had squeezed shut when he touched her and stared at him. "It's time to put that wicked tongue to good use. I have longed to feel its skill since the first time we made love."

His eyes widened. Again, her boldness shocked and delighted him. And her reward was exactly what she had demanded.

He parted her folds and pressed his lips to her. He teased with his lips, brushing along her entrance with light, playful bites. But teasing her was as tormenting to himself as it was to her. He didn't want to play, he wanted to thoroughly taste her. To delve deep inside of her. To make her come until she shook, until she was weak against the pillows and begged for his cock to finish what his tongue had begun.

Mariah couldn't stifle a harsh moan of pleasure as John drove his tongue into her sheath in earnest. He swirled his tongue around her clit, sucking the tingling bundle of nerves until she could hardly breathe from desire. She had always been exquisitely sensitive when it came to a man's mouth on her, but with John her excitement built even faster. Within just a few strokes of his tongue, she was quivering on the edge of bliss.

And when he added two thick fingers to her sheath...she was lost. She arched up with a great heaving cry and tremor after tremor of intense, focused pleasure mobbed her. She couldn't think, she couldn't speak, she couldn't breathe, all she could do was scream out as he dragged her through more and more spiraling depths of sensation.

He never slowed his pace, even as tears began to flow down her face from the intensity of the sensation. Even as she flopped back in pure exhaustion from the experience. Her body continued to twitch with each flick of his tongue and slowly, slowly he eased his pace and finally sank away from her sex to stare up at her with brown eyes almost black with desire.

"I like that," he murmured as he began to move up her trembling body. "I *like* how powerfully you react to that touch."

"I like how powerfully *you* make me react," she countered as he settled over her. He nestled between her legs and she lifted herself to rub her soaking sex against his hard length.

"Let's see if I can repeat it, yes?" he whispered.

He lowered his mouth to her and she tasted her own juices on his lips and tongue. Greedily she kissed him, her arousal rising again at the proof that he had just loved her so completely. Her heavy, heated kisses only seemed to inspire him to more.

He reached between them, fitting his cock to her entrance and glided deep inside of her in one long stroke.

John could scarcely see as stars flashed before his eyes. He had been inside a great many women in his time, but there was something about fitting himself into Mariah's body that felt...*different.* Almost like they were made for this, for each other.

He shook his head to clear it of that thought and thrust forward in the hopes that mind-blowing pleasure would make him stop waxing poetic. And it worked. His cock throbbed with every thrust into her willing and flexing body. She clung to his neck, staring up at him as her breath came in jerky pants and her hips arched with every entrance and withdrawal.

She had already experienced an explosive orgasm, but he wanted to feel her tremble around his cock, to milk him toward his own release with the tremors of her own. He drove toward that goal, rubbing his hips to hers to stimulate her tender clit, making circles with each thrust.

Sweat broke out in a thin sheen on her forehead and her gasps and moans became more erratic, proving he was doing his job. Finally, she dug her nails into his shoulders, nearly lifted her entire body from the bed and screamed out his name as her sex went wild with flutters and squeezes.

His cock swelled and he slammed into her through her crisis, even as he built toward his own. He clenched his teeth, he held his breath and then he exploded in a fiery burst of pleasure and release. Her body milked every drop of his essence from his cock and he collapsed onto her and rained soft kisses on her mouth, her cheeks, her neck.

For a moment, they lay like that, but then John flopped away from her, panting as the last vestiges of pleasure faded and left him, for the moment, satiated. This feeling never lasted, of course, but damn he did enjoy it for the short time he felt it.

Mariah rolled over and placed her head on his chest, her own breath short.

"There is one thing to be certain, we are good together," she said with a smile up at him.

He brushed stray auburn locks away from her eyes, which were bright and beautiful in the firelight. "Indeed, we are. I don't think I have ever been so swept away as I am by you."

Her eyes widened and her smile fell. "No? But you have bedded so many women."

He shrugged but said nothing else. There was nothing else to say, really.

She shifted and broke her gaze from his to stare off toward the fire for a few moments. Then she shook her head and slowly eased her body away from his. He reached for her hand.

"Where are you going?" he asked, with more desperation to his tone than he cared to think about.

She covered his hand with her own and smiled at him. "I'm dressing and then I'm returning to my townhome."

His brow wrinkled. "Returning? You aren't staying here tonight?"

She sucked in a breath and for a moment her face reflected worry and anxiety. "No," she said. "You and I are only engaged in an affair, yes?" He nodded slowly. "Then we must keep up boundaries," she said with a sigh. "I have learned that most definitely the hard way."

He stared. What did that mean?

"And your boundaries include running away the moment an encounter is finished?" he asked instead.

She lifted his fingers to her lips and pressed a gentle kiss there meant to soothe him. It didn't work, but did the exact opposite, inflamed him even more.

"It is very late," she explained. "And I think it best if I don't stay in your bed with you. It will only…complicate matters."

He pursed his lips. She was utterly correct, of course. He had never encouraged his lovers to stay with him through the night. He was always slightly annoyed if they insisted on doing so. But Mariah's refusal to remain by his side somehow…irked him.

She slipped away and gathered her things. She fastened her buttons and buckled her slippers with swiftness and efficiency he really didn't care for in that moment.

Mariah smiled as she finished closing her last button. John

continued to lounge on the bed, hoping to remain nonchalant when he felt anything but. Keyed up and filled with tension that had nothing to do with sex was more like it.

"Goodbye, John," she murmured as she leaned over to kiss him.

He cupped her face gently and drove his tongue into her mouth, daring her not to respond, proving to her, and perhaps to himself, that she still wanted him even if she insisted on leaving him. When he released her, she staggered back on unsteady feet and he smiled. There was triumph in that, at least.

"Will I see you tomorrow?" he asked.

She blinked. "Er, yes. If you intend to be at Vivien's monthly masquerade, then you shall."

John's lips pursed. Normally he loved Vivien's parties that she held monthly during the Season. They were nights of pure debauchery.

"Yes, I'll be there."

She smiled, but there was something faded about the expression. "Then I'll see you tomorrow."

He nodded as she slipped away. But when the door shut behind her, he threw himself from the bed and began to pace restlessly. Tonight he had taken his time. Tonight he had given and received all the pleasure he knew Mariah could provide. And that should have sated his desire, faded it away.

But it hadn't. If anything, he was left feeling edgier than ever. He wanted her. Now. He wanted her all night. Every night for a week. A month. Maybe even a year.

He sank down in a chair beside the fire and rubbed his eyes. "I'm in trouble," he muttered.

And never had he believed a statement more.

CHAPTER 7

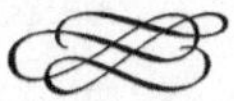

Mariah gazed around Vivien's party with a stifled sigh and her friend slipped her arm around her and squeezed.

"Don't look so thrilled," Vivien teased. "I'll think I'm putting on the soiree of the century."

Mariah smiled at Vivien. "Oh, you know you have the best fetes, my dear. My expression has nothing to do with the quality of your party."

Vivien tilted her head and Mariah could see the question perched on her friend's lips. One she did not wish to answer, so she continued swiftly.

"You know, I don't think I've ever asked you how you started having these monthly masquerades." Mariah tilted her head. "You've done them for what…three years? Since you left your last protector."

Vivien's face grew tense for a moment, but then she relaxed into a smile. "Yes, that is correct. I suppose I've always liked a masquerade. There is something so sensual about hiding behind a mask, being able to do any naughty thing with utter anonymity. I held one and it was such a huge success that the next month I held another.

And then another and another and suddenly people simply expected that there would be a monthly masquerade during the Season."

She shrugged, but Mariah didn't feel her question had been fully answered. "And what about the...*other* activities that go on during the masquerade?" she pressed.

Vivien smiled slightly. "Ah yes. The back room. Well, my home has always been a retreat for pleasure, has it not? It seemed only fitting that during a masquerade there should also be a place for the attendees to slake their needs and share their bodies."

Mariah shivered and found herself gazing around the room to find John, just as she had been all night. He was standing with two ladies, both in masks, though one had allowed hers to slip down quite low to make it clear who she was. Lord Sunderworth's mistress, a chit named Nadine or some such thing. She was a scatterbrain but pretty. Exactly the kind of woman John had taken to his bed in the past.

Mariah ground her teeth as she tried to tamp down and ignore the jealousy that was building within her.

"I see you looking at John, but you two did not arrive together. Have you had a falling out already?" Vivien asked.

Mariah turned away from him. She was being too obvious, clearly. "No, not a falling out," she said, her voice strained. "Quite the contrary, our affair is..."

She stopped. There was no use voicing how powerful their connection was. Vivien would only scold her on endangering herself and her heart. Something she was *not* doing. Intense physical connection and intense emotions could be separated.

They had to be.

"I can well imagine you two are quite good together," Vivien supplied. "But if that is true, why maintain such distance tonight?"

Mariah sighed. "I told John that I must take the first few hours of the party to continue my search for a protector. So we agreed not to come together until midnight."

Vivien looked at her evenly for a long moment. "You realize it is quarter to midnight right now."

Mariah nodded. She had been well aware of every slide of the clock's hand throughout the entire evening.

"And I don't think I've seen you talk to more than a few men during the time you've been here," Vivien continued.

Mariah swallowed. "Yes. Well, I have been *particular* in my choice of companions tonight, that is true."

Vivien arched a brow. "Particular. Yes, that is one way to put it. Another is that you have no interest in any of them. I can see you looking for a way to escape any time you are forced to be alone with any man in this room. And your eye has been wandering to John all night. When he stands with women, you look as though you'd like to slap someone. When he stands with men, you are disinterested."

Mariah shook her head. "Untrue on all accounts, Vivien."

"I've been doing this for years, Mariah. I know what I see." Her friend caught her hands. "My dearest, I hate to point out the obvious, but there is still a game afoot here for you. John may be a worthy distraction, but if he will not protect you—"

Mariah jerked her hands away and reached for a drink from the nearest footman's tray. She downed it in one swig. "I know, I know!"

Vivien stared at her, her gaze utterly focused on Mariah's face. Her friend was reading her. Analyzing her. Judging her. And as much as Mariah hated it, she wondered what the far more experienced Vivien's conclusions were. Certainly it was beginning to become harder to judge herself, perhaps she needed an outside opinion to really see what she should do.

Finally, her friend patted her arm. "My dear, you should go to him."

Mariah's eyes went wide and she staggered back a step in disbelief. "What? What happened to concerns and maintaining distance and needing a protector and all your other lectures?"

Vivien smiled. "I stand by all my sermons. But there is something between you and John that has not yet been purged from your systems. And until it is, you shall be worthless to look for a new situation for yourself. So go to him, drown yourself in what he offers. One night won't change much for you in your search. And if other men see you are the object of John's attention, that can only garner you more interest amongst them."

Mariah shifted. She didn't particularly like the idea of being with John for such a mercenary cause, but she shoved that aside. The fact was, she was being given permission to fly to his side and wrap herself in his passion. Something she wanted more than anything.

"But—" she began.

Vivien turned her around and gently shoved her in John's direction. "Go! We will speak at length about the dangers and questions later. For now just go before you make yourself sick from trying to pretend you aren't interested."

Mariah did as her friend ordered, gliding through the crowd toward John. She thought she might have heard someone say her name, but didn't stop to seek out the person. All she could see was her friend, her lover, standing a few feet away, waiting for her. And as she moved closer, it was like she had been made lighter by each step. Lighter by the fact that she would be with John tonight.

Consequences be damned.

～

John had been pretending he wasn't tracking Mariah's every movement throughout the night, but he had been. Any man who stood near her had earned John's scorn and he had been counting every moment until the offender left her side. When any one seemed to garner her attention longer than another, his heart leapt, and not in a pleasant fashion.

But now she moved toward him, a smile on her face that was just for him, and he caught his breath in anticipation of the moment she would reach his side.

He stepped away from his companion, who was midway through another empty sentence, and reached for Mariah's hand.

"Good evening," he said softly.

She smiled up at him, almost shy in her expression. "John."

He wanted to kiss her, right there in the middle of Vivien's ball-room. An act of claiming that he would normally never perform so publicly.

But before he could do something so telling and so foolish, the lady he had been standing with stepped between them.

"Why, Mariah!" Nadine said. "I had no idea you were here tonight."

Mariah pursed her lips and John could see she didn't like the other mistress. "Hello, Nadine. How *is* Lord Sunderworth?"

John could hear a not-so-subtle reminder in the way Mariah said the other man's name and he stifled a smile. So she had been watching him with other women too, and disliking what she saw just as much as he had. Her jealousy should have been distasteful to him, but it wasn't in the slightest.

Nadine shrugged. "Fine, as always. He is floating about here somewhere tonight. We have agreed to find new partners for our fun and meet later. I was hoping John would be interested in joining us."

John cast a quick glance at Mariah, who seemed to be holding her breath. On any other night in the past, he probably would have said yes. Nadine was a pretty girl and Sunderworth had good taste, so he would probably pick an equally beautiful partner who John would also get to share. Any other night, that kind of empty erotic encounter would have seemed perfectly palatable.

Tonight, it did not.

"I'm afraid I have other plans," he murmured, locking gazes with Mariah. "Though I do appreciate the offer."

Nadine looked between them and sudden understanding dawned in her blank eyes. "Ah. I see. Well, then I have wasted my time here. Good evening."

She turned on her heel and stomped away into the crowd, leaving Mariah and John alone.

"You didn't wish to take her offer?" Mariah asked in soft surprise.

John shook his head. "No. The only person I want to be with is—"

He broke the sentence off and stepped away from Mariah. What the hell was he saying? Certainly he *had* been bewitched by her eyes if he was about to admit that he wanted no one but her. That wasn't true. It couldn't be. He didn't want only one woman. He never had and he never would.

But now Mariah stared at him, golden stare flickering with questions and confusions. She knew his intention, even if he had bitten off the words. But he couldn't be that close to her. He wouldn't be.

He leaned in and struggled to return to his normal nonchalant, erotic self.

"My dear, I believe we should retire to Vivien's back room. I simply did not wish to do so with Nadine, as she has never been a favorite with me."

Vivien blinked, tilting her head to explore his face as even more confusion clouded her expression. "I—you wish to go to the back room?"

He nodded. "Of course. It is the most erotic area of Vivien's home."

She swallowed. "I see. Well, if that is your desire, I'll go with you."

He wrinkled his brow. She sounded as if they were going to be going to the hangman's noose together, not to a sensual playground. But he wasn't going to ask her about her feelings, nor was he going to share his. That was the bargain he had made with her and had already come dangerously close to betraying tonight.

He held out his elbow and for a brief moment she hesitated, but then slipped her hand into the crook. She allowed him to lead her through the ballroom and down a hallway that twisted and turned past many parlors and sitting rooms. Inside, John could hear the cries and moans of pleasure from those who had forgone the back room and decided to take their desires to a more private place.

For a moment, he considered going to one of those rooms to repeat what they had done that first night together. But he didn't. He had come too close to Mariah tonight. The best way to maintain distance, while still being able to touch and pleasure her, was the back room. It was the only way.

A large door loomed before them and as John opened it, it revealed a big, open chamber. There was no furniture in the middle of the room, which was surrounded by a low wall lined on the outside by benches. Comfortable cushions covered in silk, satin and velvet were scattered around the floor in the center.

And in the middle of this odd room ten people milled about. Kissing, touching, moaning in erotic bliss as they pleasured and shared each other in varying ways.

On the benches outside the circle, individuals and couples watched the action. There were couples grinding against each other as they stared at the sexual fascination in the middle and one couple had even begun fondling each other blatantly as they stared.

For the moment, John ignored it all and guided Mariah around the perimeter of the room to a bench in the corner that offered a good view of the center of the room, but was hidden in shadow to give its occupants the highest degree of privacy. As he motioned to the bench, Mariah blinked at him in surprise.

"I—" she whispered. "I thought you were going to tell me we must go to the middle of the circle."

Her voice was low, but John could hear the strain to it. She hadn't liked the concept that he would ask her to join the others in the center of the room, to be pleasured and touched by strangers as the others watched them. And it wasn't a generic dislike that showed on her face in the soft lights that glowed from the center of the room to highlight the lovers there. It was something more specific.

But he didn't ask her why. This was not the time, nor the place. He simply motioned to the middle of the room and the lovers there.

There were six men and four women in the circle. Some still wore their masquerade masks, but a few had removed them to reveal one of the most powerful earls in the kingdom, a widow who was highly respected by those in her charity circle and a gentleman who had risen to power through shrewd business dealings. In this instance, though, they were nothing but writhing bodies, gliding against each other.

If any of them had come in pairs, their couples had been altered. There was no rhyme or reason to the way they touched. It was just hands gliding over skin, pumping cocks, fingering slits as moans and sighs echoed through the room.

Beside him, John heard Mariah's breath catch and he looked at her out of the corner of his eye. She leaned forward to get a closer look, her hands curling over the edge of the wall that separated those who watched from those who fucked. Her body betrayed her arousal. Through her thin silk gown, he saw her puckered nipples, he heard her rough breathing, he saw the way she squirmed as she watched one of the women before them straddle one man's lips so that he could eat her tender pussy while she sucked another man's cock deep into her throat.

Mariah's arousal increased his own. He slipped around to stand behind her and wrapped his arms around her to drag her against his chest. She shivered and pushed her backside against his cock, rotating her hips against his. He moaned against her ear and began to kiss and lick the column of her throat, reveling in how her body grew warmer with his touch.

In the center of the room, the foreplay had ceased and now the couples joined in earnest. One of the women had taken a man deep within her backside and another pushed into her pussy. With each stroke of one cock or the other, the three participants gasped and moaned with pleasure. The final four, two men and two women, were just as busy. The two men took turns stroking and licking one woman's pussy while she busily fingered the final woman's sex in time to their ministrations.

Mariah stared, mesmerized, it seemed, by the erotic visions before her. So mesmerized that when John touched her, she jumped with surprise.

"Forget I was here?" he asked with a smile.

She shook her head. "I could never do that, I assure you," she whispered. She leaned up close to his ear. "I want you."

He blinked in surprise at her bold admission. He had planned, of course, to tease her while they watched. To tempt her. Perhaps even to take her if she could be persuaded, but now she took control of the situation, demanding.

She turned into his chest and leaned up to kiss him. The kiss was deep as she swirled her tongue around his, sucking him in as she rubbed her body against his.

"Please," she murmured.

He didn't have to be asked twice. He spun her around so that they could both watch the group in the circle again. Couples had traded off now, women were riding men, taking their cocks deep within their throats. One of the men was thrusting deep within a shaking woman while another man positioned himself behind him to take him at the same time. There were no taboos, nothing but pleasure.

"Hurry," she groaned and he lifted her skirts up around her waist.

He tore at his fly until his cock was free and then glided deep into her sheath. She pushed back against him as she flexed her sex and gripped him in heated, slick heaven. They slammed against each other as they continued to watch the orgy in the center of the room.

Others watched them too, even though they were in the deepest shadows. John saw the eyes flit to them with excitement, saw the other couples moving together in much the same way. It only increased his desire, his longing to make Mariah cry out with pleasure as she found release.

He cupped her hips and drove harder, circling and coaxing her pleasure higher and higher.

She tensed against him at last and made a deep, guttural cry as her orgasm hit her. He slammed through it, building toward his own until finally he gasped and pure pleasure pumped through him and deep into her body.

They stood like that for a few moments, panting together as the scene in the center of the chamber continued to play out. Then John straightened up, smoothed Mariah's skirts back over her body and buttoned his fly. She turned to look at him with an almost shy smile. He reached out to take her hand.

"Would you like to return to the ballroom?"

She nodded. "I think the purpose has been served, has it not?"

He glanced at the center of the room where the throng of naked bodies was still writhing. "For us, I believe it has."

He escorted her around the perimeter of the room, past the other couples outside the wall who were now also making love with abandon and into the hallway. He shut the door behind them, but the sounds of sex and sin continued to echo down the hall as they walked toward the ballroom.

CHAPTER 8

Mariah's body continued to tremble and tingle as John maneuvered them back into the ballroom where the masquerade went on as normal. Only Mariah felt anything but.

There was nothing like sex with John. It always left her both satisfied and anticipating the next encounter. She had no idea how to label what they were experiencing, but she didn't want it to stop.

As he took two drinks from the tray of a passing footman and held one out to her, she smiled.

"Just what I needed," she said with a laugh. "But then, you do seem to always know what that is."

He also smiled, but the expression was muted, as if heavier thoughts plagued his mind.

"Did you ever watch before?" he asked her as he restlessly ran a thumb back and forth over the edge of his glass.

She blinked. She hadn't expected him to wish to return to the topic of what they'd just done. She was no innocent, to be certain, but normally one didn't analyze or discuss those sorts of things. At least, not in the middle of a ballroom, even Vivien's.

"Watch like we did tonight?" she asked. When he nodded, she

pressed further. "Owen has only been gone for a few weeks, I haven't had the time, to be honest."

He frowned at her obvious avoidance of the topic. "I meant when you were with Owen."

She couldn't help but draw back in surprise. John *never* asked her about her relationship with Owen. Not when Owen was alive, and certainly not since his death. In fact, John had made it perfectly clear that he didn't *want* to know what she and his friend had shared in their bed or anywhere else.

And yet now he pressed her on those very delicate topics. She flinched at the memory of Owen and his desires. But the pain at his loss was beginning to become muted partly due to his actions toward her...and partly because of John's.

"Yes," she admitted softly. "I'm sure you must know that Owen always liked to watch."

John arched a brow. "It seemed tonight that you enjoyed that equally."

She shrugged but felt anything but dismissive on the topic. John was probing a very personal and painful arena of her life. One she did not wish to reveal. Nonchalance was her only weapon.

"I did. I do. It is most stimulating, especially when there is such abandon as there was tonight."

She shivered just thinking about it, and John shifted as if he too was thinking of what they'd seen and done.

"And yet when I first suggested the back room, you hesitated in going," he pressed. "I felt high emotion in you, and not of the pleasant variety. Is there a reason?"

Mariah closed her eyes and drew a calming breath. John was a bulldog on topics he pursued. Now that he had gotten hold of this one, she could see he wouldn't release it until he had the answers he demanded.

"John," she said softly. "You are the one who did not wish to be my protector, who wanted to keep our affair so rigidly free of connection. Why the shift now?"

He stared at her in plain disbelief.

"Mariah," he whispered. "I am not so cold as you accuse. The fact is I am not asking you these questions as a protector or a lover. I ask you because I am your friend. I'm still that, aren't I?"

Once he had told her they'd never been friends because of his lust for her, but she'd always known that was a statement meant to make a point, not truth.

"You are my friend," she replied, her voice so soft that he had to lean closer to hear her.

He smiled and the expression was genuine with relief and affection. "Then tell me, why did the beginning of tonight make you so uncomfortable? I don't want to repeat that if I can avoid it."

Mariah took a deep breath. Damn him for seducing not her body, but her emotions. For making her trust him, when she knew she shouldn't, friendship and passion be damned.

"I—" she began, trying to keep her mind from wandering to unpleasant memories. It was an impossible task. "Owen *did* love to watch, as did I. Our shared desire for such a thing brought us closer at first. But after a while he told me that watching was not enough to satisfy him. He wanted us to…participate."

John's eyes went wide and he nearly dropped the drink in his hand.

"Participate?" he repeated as if he didn't understand.

She knew the feeling. When Owen had suggested it, she had barely understood herself.

"He…said that we had been together a long while, two years the first time he brought up the subject," she continued with difficulty. "And that our passion was growing *stale*."

She spit the last word out with difficulty, for hearing it had hurt her so deeply. Owen had been kind in the exchange, but no amount of kindness could ease the pain of his meaning.

John tensed but said nothing, so she continued.

"He asked me to come with him to the center of the back room, to give myself over to whatever the others wished, and he would do the same. I refused. I could not picture myself in the middle of that room, watching my lover pleasure and be pleasured by others. I wasn't ready for such a shift in our relationship. I knew it would open a Pandora's box."

"And what did Owen say when you refused him?" John pressed in a thin, tight voice that betrayed unexpected anger at the subject.

She blushed. "He did not force me, but he made it very clear that he was disappointed to his core. Disappointed in me and my 'missish refusal to tend to his desires'."

John cursed beneath his breath. "I assume the subject did not drop, either."

She shook her head. "No. Soon after he began suggesting we recruit a friend or two of his to join us in the privacy of our rooms, rather than begin with such a public act. He even suggested you."

John backed up another step. The anger that had been mild in his tone now flashed dark and deep in his eyes.

"Me?" he repeated, his voice gruff and low.

She blinked. "You sound surprised."

He laughed, but there was no humor to the sound. "I am."

She shook her head. "I—I thought you knew! That he had talked to you about the subject and had your permission to bring up the topic with me."

"No," he barked and several heads pivoted at the harsh sound. "No. I'm sorry, Mariah. I must leave."

She opened her mouth to respond, to question, but he gave her no opportunity. He turned on his heel and marched from the ballroom, leaving her alone, confused and hurt in a way she had not felt in weeks.

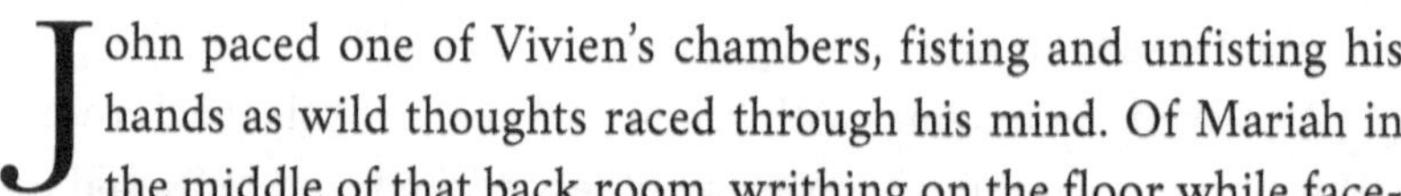

John paced one of Vivien's chambers, fisting and unfisting his hands as wild thoughts raced through his mind. Of Mariah in the middle of that back room, writhing on the floor while faceless others pleasured her. Of Owen putting her in that place. Of Owen sharing her with other men…with *him*.

The images were as troubling as they were titillating and he could not seem to control his anger and frustration as they bubbled up again and again, each time stronger.

The door behind him opened and he pivoted, thinking he would find Mariah there, come to look for him after his abrupt departure. Instead, Vivien stood in the doorway, arms folded, staring at him.

"Not now," he growled, but she entered anyway and shut the door behind her.

"Out with it," Vivien said, her voice low as she sank into the nearest settee and stared at him. "What is going on with you?"

John drew a few deep breaths. He knew what she meant by her open question. This behavior was not like him. He didn't show emotion. He didn't inspire people to inquire after his wellbeing. He shook his head.

"Nothing," he managed to grind out through clenched teeth that belied his statement entirely.

Vivien pursed her lips. "I see. Nothing. Is that your answer to *me*?"

He paced away from her and stared at the fire. "It is my answer to everyone because it is the truth."

Vivien folded her arms. "I have known you a long time, John. I've never seen you like this."

He turned to face Vivien, a woman he had counted as a friend for a handful of years. Probably the only woman he could truly call that name. Even Mariah inspired far more complex attachments than mere friendship.

"Did you know Owen wished to share Mariah? In the back room? With his friends? With *me*?" he snapped out.

Vivien hesitated, then nodded. "Yes. Mariah told me."

He slammed a hand on the mantel. "How could he do that? If he loved her, how could he do that?"

Vivien pushed to her feet and tilted her head to stare at him.

"Because he did *not* love her. You were his closest friend—surely that can come as no surprise to you. He told her he did, he treated her well enough. But love her? I doubt it."

John squeezed his eyes shut. When Vivien put it so succinctly, it was true. Owen never talked about Mariah when she was not in the room. It was always John who had brought her up as a topic of conversation. Owen's eye had never stopped roaming. And in the last days of his life, he had even begun to talk about marrying to produce his heirs. When John asked him about Mariah, Owen made it obvious he had never considered her in the decision. He would only say it would work out...somehow.

"But she loved him," he said softly.

Vivien wrinkled her brow. "Mariah is not built for this lifestyle. She had one lover before Owen and then stayed with your friend for three years. She never took any offers for protectors higher up the chain of influence. Was that because she has some deep, abiding love for Owen? Or that in order to allow herself to perform the acts expected of a mistress, she must tell herself she is in love?"

John shook his head without hesitation. "No. I refuse to believe her to be dishonest with her heart. She did care for him, I know that to be true. She mourns him."

"Oh, do not misunderstand me. I don't claim her to be dishonest with her heart. She convinces herself, more than anyone else, that her feelings are real," Vivien agreed. "She does mourn Owen. The accident that took his life was hideous. And she cared for him. But I do not think she was as satisfied during their time together as she has told herself, and others, that she was."

John pursed his lips. "And do you think that is true about her experience with me, as well? Is all her connection to me merely an act to induce her to take to my bed?"

Vivien's expression was unreadable at his question. "I'm amazed you would care. You don't want her beyond a few nights, a few weeks at best."

He sucked in a breath. Everyone kept saying that, including himself, but it didn't ring true. He shook the thought away.

"No one likes being lied to," he snapped.

Vivien was silent for a moment. "Then allow me to ease your ruffled feelings. I do think things are different between you. There is no need for her to force something between you. She wants you quite passionately. More to the point, she has a true regard and respect for you, and clearly you two satisfy each other greatly."

Vivien moved toward him. "John, she is my best friend. Probably the only true friend I have in this world. And I think the idea that you are presenting her with an affair that is only for her pleasure is a great one, indeed. She deserves that. But…"

John tilted his head. "But?"

"This conversation, along with my own observations, makes me wonder…what *are* your true feelings for her?"

John tensed. True feelings? He could have no true feelings for her. For anyone.

When he was silent, Vivien continued, "Because you know as well as I do that she has suffered a great pain, believing she was loved and learning that was far from true. She dismisses it as if it does not affect her, but she is hurt and humiliated. I would not want her to be lured in by your kindness and your affection, only to have you withdraw it. I think with you…with you it would do more damage."

John swallowed. How that could be true, he did not know. But he refused to think about it, to face it.

"That shall not happen," he said, his voice cracking. "Because I have no feelings toward Mariah beyond a friendship we have shared for three years and a desire to have her."

Vivien was silent for a moment, but then she nodded. "If that is true, or if that is the truth you choose to repeat, then be certain she knows it now. Otherwise you will end up doing more harm than good later. And Mariah deserves better."

John nodded. "That is one thing we can agree on, Vivien. Mariah deserves far better. Than Owen could give her. Or that I can."

Vivien's lips parted, but she did not stop him when he left the room, left her home, passed his waiting carriage and walked off into the dark night. To look for trouble. To look for a way to forget.

CHAPTER 9

Mariah shifted as her carriage rounded another corner, but her discomfort had nothing to do with her current mode of transportation. Her destination was what made her stomach flutter and her heart race.

She was heading to John's home.

Normally that fact would not cause her such anxiety. After all, she had been to his home many times in the past without the thought of it making her weak. Everything was different now. It had been three days since his abrupt departure from Vivien's masquerade. Three days since they made love or talked. He had sent her no word during that time, offered her no explanation for his avoidance.

If he was ending this affair, she deserved to hear it from his lips. She refused to sit around, moping as she waited. She had done that very thing with Owen for years and had learned her lesson.

With John, if she wanted something, she was going to follow Vivien's advice and take it.

The carriage stopped and all her bravado faded as the footman came around to open the door for her.

"Should we wait on the drive, miss?" her driver asked.

She shook her head. "No. I—I am not certain how long I will be.

Feel free to take your rest in the servant area and I will ring for you when I am ready."

Of course, she could be utterly humiliated if John refused to see her…or worse, dismissed her within moments of her arrival, but she was willing to take that risk. She hoped it wouldn't come to that.

Those hopes troubled her as she strode up to the door and rapped loudly. It was only seconds before Swanson opened it and stared down at her with a blank expression perfected by only the servants of highest caliber.

"Miss Desmond," he said with the slightest hint of a smile. "May I help you?"

"I do not have an appointment," she said, repeating the words she had been practicing all the carriage ride over. "But I demand to see Mr. Rycroft. Now."

The butler's brows lifted in what was probably his first expression of surprise in a decade or more. But he motioned her into the house and to a parlor.

"I shall ascertain if Mr. Rycroft is currently in residence, of course. And pass along the urgency of your request."

He left her alone and Mariah began to pace.

"It wasn't a request," she muttered to no one but herself. "It was a rather strenuous order, I think."

Time slipped by slowly, though each time Mariah looked at the clock on the mantel, it had only moved one little space to indicate a minute's passage. It was less than five of those minutes, which felt like an hour, when the door behind her opened again.

She turned, half-expecting to see Swanson back to dismiss her, and went weak in the knees when it was John himself standing there. He stared at her, speechless, for what seemed like another eternity. Then he shut the door and stepped forward.

"Mariah," he breathed. "I—I did not expect to see you here today."

She arched a brow as all the emotion she had been keeping in check rushed to the surface at once. "Truly, this is how you address me? You did not expect to see me? You ignore what happened a few days ago and you pretend you have not cut me out of your life since?"

John shifted. "I'm sorry, Mariah, I did not mean to be flip in my response. I realize our last meeting ended awkwardly."

"To say the least," she muttered.

A shadow of a smile crossed his lips at her daring attitude and Mariah's heart lodged in her throat at the sight. Oh why did his appearance have to undo her so? Why could she not be stronger? She was a courtesan, after all, not some inexperienced girl.

"I'm sorry," he said and she jolted.

In three years, she was not certain Owen had ever said he was sorry to her. He bought her trinkets when she was upset, but admitting he was wrong was not his strong suit. Why had she not questioned him more? Demanded a higher level of respect from him?

"You are?" she asked, her thoughts returning to the man before her.

He nodded. "I should not have stormed out of the masquerade as I did. I cannot explain it."

She pursed her lips. "Cannot or will not?"

He stared at her for a moment, then shrugged one shoulder. "Take your pick, Mariah."

Her warmth at his apology faded and she folded her arms in frustration. "John, you are a mystery. You pretend joviality, but I sense your anger and frustration, both in general and when it comes to me."

He shifted and his lips grew thinner with each word, manifesting proof of exactly what she had just said.

"Do you demand an explanation for this?" he asked, raising his hands in aggravation. "We have agreed again and again, Mariah, we are in an affair, not a relationship. I owe you no explanations."

She shook her head. "An unfair claim when you continue to have your ire raised about subjects that pertain to me. A prime example is when I said Owen offered to share me with you. You turned purple with what can only be described as rage and you abandoned me in the middle of a ballroom. How can I not be expected to be curious about why you do these things?"

He turned away, his hand clenching and unclenching at his side even as he struggled to remain calm. "There are things about me you do not know, Mariah. You can never know. If they perturb you, I am sorry, but they are what they are. And I am who I am."

She should have backed away, but there was such an undercurrent of pain to his face, to his voice, to the way his shoulders were thrown back as if he anticipated an attack, that she could not.

"And I am who I am," she said, this time softer. "Part of who I am as a mistress is a comfort. I want to help you—"

He spun on her. "But you are not my mistress, Mariah."

She flinched. "A fact you continually remind me of, I don't know how I can keep forgetting."

When he did not respond to her barb, she sighed. "At the ball, you asked me to tell you of my feelings because of our friendship. Does that friendship not go both ways, despite whatever you've said to me about the desire you felt for me from the past?"

He shook his head. "I don't know."

"Yes, you do!" She grasped his hands. "You cannot deny that we *have* been friends. Would you deny me the comfort I could offer you in that realm?"

He tilted his head as he examined her face so very closely and carefully. It was almost like he was judging her, playing out the telling of whatever secrets he held and pretending any response she might give.

But as he hesitated and fought whatever war was in his heart, she couldn't help but see how deep his pain went. It was odd how she'd never seen it before, but little by little it grew plainer to her. Almost like she was peeling back his protective layers to find his true self buried there.

"Mariah, there is so much," he began.

She leaned forward, anxious to hear whatever small part of his past he would share, when there was a knock at the door behind them.

Both of them froze and then slowly, John turned to the door. "Come in," he croaked, his tone a mixture of relief and disappointment.

The chamber door opened and Swanson stood in the hallway. But it wasn't the normally unflappable Swanson who never reacted. Now he was pale and his lips thin.

"I'm sorry to interrupt, sir," he said. "But…your—your brother is here."

Mariah pivoted to stare at John in utter surprise. She had never heard him speak of his family. She had never even known he *had* a brother. And from the shocked and horrified expression on his face, this arrival was not one he expected or desired.

And the layers peeled a little further, revealing a very complicated man who she very much wished to comfort. Even though he would not allow it. Even though she should not do it.

John's ears rang and his vision seemed a little blurry as he stared without blinking at his butler and tried to digest these words that seemed so foreign to him.

"I—what?" he asked, needing to hear it again. Not wanting to hear it, but *needing* to hear it.

Swanson's expression, which rarely changed, grew a little gentler as he said, "Your *brother*, sir. Mr. Adam Rycroft."

John nodded. That was what he thought he'd heard. Knew he'd heard. But he needed the repetition to be sure he wasn't in some strange dream.

"Show him to my office. I will be there shortly."

Swanson bowed out of the chamber. "Yes, sir."

As the door shut behind his servant, John paced to the window to stare out onto the street below. There was a gloomy, spitting rain streaking the glass and that fit his mood entirely. But before he could grow too maudlin, Mariah touched him.

It was a simple touch, really, just the brush of her fingers on his arm to urge him to face her, but her skin was warm and her face filled with empathy, not pity, as she stared up at him.

"John," she began softly. "Your brother?"

He jerked out a nod. "Yes. We...we have been estranged for years. I don't know why he's here, Mariah."

He heard the plaintive quality to his tone and cursed himself for showing such weakness. But Mariah didn't react except to slide her hand from his arm to cup his cheek. She smoothed her fingers there gently.

"What can I do, John? What can I do?"

He stared down at her and a wild desire filled him. To tell her everything about himself, to confess his sins and his sorrows. To take her hand and run with her as fast and as far as he could.

But the moment passed and he instead cupped her chin and lifted her face to his. He pressed a kiss to her mouth, tasting her, letting the feel of her lips calm him.

"Nothing," he whispered in answer to her question as he pulled away with great reluctance. "You can do nothing. But thank you for wanting to try."

She looked up at him with a hint of sad frustration. "Should I wait for you?"

He shook his head. "No. Go home. I have no idea how long this will be and I doubt I'll be in the mood for company once it's over."

Her lips parted to protest, but then she stepped back and nodded. Her expression was grim and there was a glimmer of hurt in her stare, but she simply said, "Very well, John. If that is your wish."

She began to move past him, but then caught his hand. She squeezed gently as she looked up into his face. "If you need me, you know I'll be waiting for you."

John stared at her. She had never said as much before, but in reality he *did* know that. He could depend on Mariah, even at his worst. Even if he didn't want to depend on anyone.

He smiled, but she didn't wait for his response. She simply slipped away and left him as he had asked her to do. Alone. And he felt utterly alone as he stared at the door she left open in her wake and tried to ready himself to see his brother.

But there was no readying for this encounter. There was nothing but anxiety and pain.

CHAPTER 10

John stared at the door to his office a fraction too long before he took a deep breath and opened it. He took only one step inside when he skidded to a stop to stare at the man standing at the fireplace with a faraway look in his eyes. The eyes John shared with him, along with a painful history.

"Adam," he croaked out, his voice breaking just a fraction.

His brother turned from the fire with a jump and the two men gaped at each other as if they were strangers. He could see Adam's hesitation ran as deep as his own. But then, they'd never really known how to be brothers to each other. Their father had ensured that.

"John," he finally managed to say in a choked tone.

He moved from the fireplace and held out a hand. They shook and John flinched at the scar that slashed across Adam's hand. He'd almost forgotten that one. It was a punishment from their father for some crime. He had a few of his own.

Desperate to ease the awkward tension, John shut the door behind him and motioned to the chair across from his desk.

"Please, sit," he said as he came around to the other side of the desk and took his own place. "Would you like a drink?"

Adam shook his head. "No, no thank you."

John stared at the man seated across from him. His brother was a handsome man, there was no denying that. But instead of spiraling into a life of debauchery, as John had decided to do, he had taken a far more straight-laced path. A path their father had chosen, just as he had chosen Adam.

John settled back in his chair. "I am surprised to see you here, brother. It's been a long time."

Adam nodded. "Yes. Four years. Since our last argument about who else? Our father."

John pursed his lips at his brother's bitter tone. He felt his own share of bitterness at the thought. The argument that had finally severed them had been ugly. The words, the actions, the fact they'd come to blows...all of those facts were ones John tried not to remember.

"You were right," Adam all but whispered.

John jerked back to attention. "Right?"

Adam rose from his chair and paced the room restlessly.

"You and I always dealt with our father differently, didn't we?" he asked as he glanced at John over his shoulder. "You saw evil in his every action, while I desperately searched for good."

John kept his mouth shut, but it was a proper assessment. Often he had envied his brother his ability to forgive, to search for something John knew wasn't there. To continue to love their father despite his very deep and dangerous failings.

Adam sighed. "Even when we last spoke, it was just after Father told me I was to inherit his entire fortune. You warned me that it was a power play, but I insisted on giving him the benefit of the doubt. I wanted to believe that his abusiveness was all the in the past." He faced John and there was heartache on his face. "It was not."

John squeezed his eyes shut. "I'm sorry, Adam. I take no pleasure in hearing that."

Adam shrugged. "I allowed him to come between us for years, but the very least I can do now is try to protect you. To warn you."

John sat up straighter. "Warn me? Of what?"

His brother sank back into his seat and leaned over the desk. "Father has put his sights back on you."

Bile rose in John's throat as he stared at his brother. "What? Why?"

Adam shook his head and turned his eyes away from his brother. "I finally defied him one too many times. He has cut me off entirely and will soon darken your doors to tell you he intends to give you everything. But you know that everything comes at a very high price, indeed."

"No." John rose from his seat. "I want nothing to do with him and his inheritance. I have worked very hard to create my own fortune so I would not have to depend upon his 'grace'."

"You know that doesn't matter," Adam said with a blank expression that was more telling than any emotion would have been. Their father had broken him. "He will come and keep coming. If he must destroy you to get you under his thumb, he will make every attempt to do so."

"Yes," John said, his tone flat to his own ears. "There is no denying that is true."

The bile in his throat threatened to rise farther, but he swallowed it down, just as he was forced to swallow down this news.

Adam rose from his seat and moved toward him a step before he stopped, hesitant. "I am sorry. So sorry for everything, John. But I wanted to warn you if I could."

John stared at his brother. He could see the strain the past few years had taken. Although Adam was two years his younger, he looked older at present. Drawn out. Pained.

"Thank you," he said softly. "Thank you for coming here. I assume doing so has put you at risk."

"Oh yes." Adam shook his head. "I'm certain I shall be punished in some way. Although what more he can take, I shudder to imagine."

"Is there anything I can do?"

Adam shook his head. "Just forgive me for taking his side. For being so naïve and blind to his true self."

"There is nothing to forgive," John reassured him. Certainly, he had blamed his brother over the years, but seeing him now… He could feel no anger toward him, only pity. And a wish that everything could have been different between them.

Adam smiled slightly, almost as if he could read John's mind. "I have missed you."

John drew back. These deeper emotions were not easy for him, after all he had spent a lifetime being punished for their display, but what he felt was stronger than what he feared. With a grim nod, he said, "I have missed you too."

His brother glanced at him in surprise, but then he smiled and John saw in his eyes the brother he'd once known.

"I've been under his thumb for so long," Adam said. "I might be able to help *you*."

"You mean to report all his plans to me and play spy?" John asked.

Adam flinched, but then nodded. "Something to that effect, yes."

John shook his head. "No, I am better than him. I would not ask that of you."

Adam drew back in surprise that cut John to his core. His brother had been so removed from kindness for so long, he could hardly understand it now.

"Where are you staying, for I assume he removed you from the house he provided?" John pressed.

"Oh yes." Adam laughed. "I have been summarily thrown into the gutter. But I have let a small home with the monies I secreted away for years."

John shifted. "I could help. I think I have a place for you in one of my ventures."

Adam's brow wrinkled. "I did not come here for your charity."

John shook his head. "We've spent years being pitted against each other. If you'd like the opportunity, I am certain it would be much better to work together. Think about it and stop by in a few days to give me your answer."

His brother rose again and held out a hand. "I will. Thank you, John."

John took the hand. Already his brother's handshake seemed stronger. "Thank you. For taking this risk. I appreciate the warning more than you know."

But as his brother left the room, John sank back into his chair. The warning gave him time, but he knew his father. Nothing would prevent Vaughn Rycroft from making the attempt to take what he wanted. He could only hope it was an attempt that would fail. But until it was over, nothing was safe and there would be no escaping.

Except with one woman, who he needed to see, to touch, more than ever.

~

Mariah paced her bedchamber. Her restless steps made her nightshift sweep around her ankles, but she did not bother to lift her hem or slow her stride. She couldn't. All she could do was think of John.

It had been hours since she left him in his parlor. Left him with a sick, lost look on his face that was unlike anything he had ever seen in his life.

A brother.

She had never known he had a brother. Certainly Owen had never made mention of the fact, even though they had been friends for years. But then, as she looked back on her lover with the benefit of distance, she was beginning to recognize that he hadn't really made much attempt to care about any other person, even his friend.

He undoubtedly knew about John's brother, but the separation between the men likely did nothing for Owen.

After all, the fact did not interrupt his own pleasure, so why would it matter to him?

She pursed her lips, angry at herself for having such treacherous thoughts about a man she loved. True or not, they were not kind and Owen could do nothing to defend himself against them.

She shook her head and her mind flitted back to John. This might be an affair only, but she cared for him. She refused to think about how deeply, but even if she didn't analyze further, the fact remained the same. He was in her heart, even if they could be nothing but lovers and friends.

Since she cared, she wanted to help him. But how?

Behind her, there was a light knock on her door and Mariah turned in surprise as her maid poked her head inside.

"I—I'm sorry, miss," the girl said, cheeks flaming. "I know it's late for such an intrusion, but Lymon sent me up to tell you that you have a guest."

Mariah's eyes went wide as her gaze slipped to the clock. It was nearly midnight. A very bold person her visitor must be, indeed, if the person intruded upon her so late at night.

"Who is it?" she asked, reaching for her robe.

The girl blushed deeper. "It is…it's Mr. Rycroft, miss."

Mariah paused with her robe on only half her body and stared at the girl. "Mr. Rycroft?" she repeated, her voice trembling. "Is here?"

"Yes, miss. In the parlor."

She nodded and hoped her glee and anxiety weren't too obvious a mixture on her face.

"Yes, very good. I'll be down directly."

"I'll have Lymon tell him."

As the girl left, Mariah spun on the mirror to stare at herself. Her cheeks were pink and her eyes bright with excitement. John was here. Here in her home, where he had not called for over a year. And then it had certainly had nothing to do with her. He had accompanied Owen on a brief visit and teased her mercilessly about a chair in her parlor that was done in an awful pink fabric, which she had changed directly.

Why she recalled so many details of the day, she had no idea. And now he was here, while they were in the midst of a passionate affair. Despite the fact that he had told her he did not wish to see her here. To picture her in her bed with his former best friend.

She shook her head. There was no time to think. No time to do anything but smooth her hair and rush to the door. She clung to the handrail as she scurried down the stairs at twice her normal speed and nearly put herself soundly on her ass. Somehow she made it to the parlor door, though, and skidded to a stop as she stared at the door separating her from John.

"Breathe," she whispered, then opened the parlor door and stepped inside.

She had every intention of maintaining distance, of allowing him to come to her, to share whatever was on his mind in his own time and fashion. But when she saw him standing by the fire, his eyes hollow and his lips pressed together in an unhappy line, all her intentions fled. She raced across the room to him and slipped her arms around him.

"Oh John," she whispered as she held him.

She had so much more to say, but he would not allow it. He gripped her shoulders lightly and stepped away from her just a fraction. When he looked down at her, his eyes were wild with emotion and dark with pain. Pain that touched her.

"You asked me what you could do," he said, his voice rough with desire and emotion bound together.

She nodded.

"This," he said, then dropped his mouth to hers for a hard, passionate kiss. He drove his tongue between her lips, demanding, crushing, utterly devastating in its power. She went weak, leaning against him, clinging to his shoulders as she tried to maintain some equilibrium.

An impossible task when he had begun rocking against her in a clear indication of what he would do next.

She drew back, panting, and stared up at him. "I—" she stammered, trying to clear her cloudy mind. "You want to do this...*here?*" When he nodded, she blinked. "But you said...because this was the home I shared with Owen, you didn't want..."

He turned his face as if slapped, but when he looked back at her there was no diminishment to his desire.

"I know what I said," he growled, hauling her closer. "But the last thing I am thinking of is Owen. I just want you. I—I need you."

She would have staggered back at that last admission but John held her too tightly. He stared down at her, holding her gaze with his, sucking her in to his passion and his pain until she could see nothing, feel nothing else.

"Yes," she whispered and his lips descended again.

She clung to his shoulders, dragging him closer, pouring all the comfort he would not allow her to offer into him. She tasted him, delicately at first and then with increasing passion as she pushed him toward the settee in the middle of the room.

He fell back against the pillows and stared up at her as she stepped into better light and untied her silky robe. As it fell away, he caught his breath and she couldn't help but smile.

She had always insisted upon pretty night-rails made of satin and lace. This one was no different, made from white silk with only a swatch of lace covering each breast. It clung to her curves, leaving nothing to the imagination.

"Do you like what you see, Mr. Rycroft?" she teased as she slipped a finger beneath the thin strap of the shift and teased it over her shoulder ever-so slightly.

"You know I do," he said, motioning to the swollen outline of his cock against his trouser front. "I think it is more than obvious."

"Indeed," she said, wetting her lips as she thought of taking that very cock deep inside her in some way, any way. "Why don't you loosen your trousers and free that very uncomfortable-looking erection while I too unburden myself of the confines of clothes?"

He smiled and did as she asked. His cock popped free and Mariah's eyes went wide as he immediately took himself in hand and began to stroke. Watching him pleasure himself in that way made her pussy wet and her nipples harden even further against the soft lace.

She swished her hips as she glided the night shift strap away from her shoulder and revealed one breast. He pumped his cock harder as she licked her thumb and swirled it around the tight, perfect peak.

"Fuck, Mariah," he groaned, hesitating in his self-pleasure as he squeezed his eyes shut.

She smiled and glided the opposite strap from her shoulder. Now her gown hung only from the waist down and her breasts were fully revealed.

"So pretty," he murmured.

"Thank you," she whispered and then shook her hips to force her gown into a pool at her feet. She stepped free of it, kicking it away to stand before him naked.

With a groan, he released his cock to reach for her. He caught her hip and drew her forward to rest his cheek against her hip and stroke her thigh with his opposite hand. Strong currents of pleasure shot from his fingertips, through her flesh, into her blood. They heated her body, making her sex clench and her nipples tingle.

"You make me wild," he murmured against her flesh. "Being with you is unlike any other woman."

She stared down at him, once again taken aback by his confessions. He who always behaved as if women were interchangeable cogs in his machine of pleasure. But she was special to him, and even if that feeling only lasted a moment, it still made her wild with desire and giddy with pride.

"Then let me comfort you," she whispered. "Lie back, allow for this pleasure without thought for consequence."

He jerked his gaze to her. "And what of *your* pleasure? How do I release any thought for that?"

"You don't have to worry about my pleasure," she said with a smile. "I will experience a great deal of it, I am certain."

He hesitated and then, to her surprise, he acquiesced, sinking back against the settee and staring up at her in anticipation and even a little anxiety.

Feelings she hoped she would soon put to ease, along with the pain she was certain he did not wish to reveal so clearly. She caught up a pillow from the settee and dropped it on the floor between his legs, then she knelt down between them. He caught his breath as her intentions became clear. But she didn't allow him time to direct or protest, she simply caught his heated, throbbing member and took him deep into her throat in one gliding stroke.

He gave a garbled shout as he lifted his hips to drive even farther, and she took every inch of him with pleasure. He filled her mouth with silken steel and she reveled in his taste and his reaction as she swirled her tongue around his length. She lifted up higher on her knees, clutching the base of his cock and stroking even as she glided her mouth up and down over him, taking him deeper, tasting him more completely.

~

John tried to hold back his helpless moans and cries, but it was impossible as Mariah pleasured him with her wicked, experienced mouth. She knew exactly how to test him and taste him, how tightly to hold him and suck him, to make him go wild. And he did, losing his grip on control little by little as he forgot everything except how good her mouth felt.

He lifted his hips, gripping the settee cushions in steel fists as the pleasure mounted, building toward a crescendo he wouldn't be able to halt or temper. And yet he didn't have to worry about Mariah. She knew the consequences of her actions. If her tiny, vibrating moans were any indication, she welcomed them. She glanced up at him from time to time with hazel eyes darkened by pleasure, both the given and the received.

But just as his pleasure reached its peak, she popped his cock from her lips, rose up to straddle him and dropped her slick pussy down over him in one smooth stroke.

He jolted from this new pleasure of her hot sheath, but she gave him no time to adjust. She just began to ride, hard and heavy, holding his shoulders as she arched her back and flexed her hips over him.

He loved how she didn't wait for him to give her release, but rubbed her clitoris over him to find it herself. And how she didn't blush or pretend she was an innocent, but reveled in her own sensual power.

He gripped her hips and lifted to meet her strokes, leaning forward to suck one hard nipple as she rode him. She gasped out a sound of surprise and pleasure and then her hips went mad as orgasm gripped her. Her sheath flexed against him in out-of-control tremors and it was too much. He exploded inside of her with a grunt that rang in his ears and made the world around him blur quite beautifully.

He didn't know how long they sat, bodies still intertwined, heads pressed together, breathing matched, but finally she sat up and stared down at him with a tiny smile.

"Amazing," she whispered. "You and I knew each other for years, and yet we never did this. How much we were missing."

John stared at her. In those years, she had been bound to his best friend. In love with him, or so she'd always said, and he knew she had been a faithful and true companion to Owen.

But her words sparked images of something amazing. Of the two of them together all this time. Doing this. Sharing their bodies, but also more. And he realized he didn't want to let her go after a brief affair. He *wanted* to be her protector. He wanted to know that she would be there in the morning when he woke, that she would be on his arm. That he could turn to her for companionship and comfort, and offer the same for her.

The realization shocked him. He had always taken such pride in the fact that he never bound himself to anyone. Deeper bonds never seemed to result in anything good. But now...now he couldn't escape this desire.

But he was also not ready to voice it. Not until he could practice his words, make sure they did not promise too much...nor too little.

So instead, he cupped the back of her head and drew her down for a kiss. Not a passionate possession, but something else. He tasted her and felt differently, knowing she would be his. He held her and reveled in how perfectly she fit his arms and his body. And she would be there, for as long as he desired.

"Are you well?" she asked as he pulled away.

He cocked his head. "Well? Yes, of course. Why do you ask?"

She shrugged. "There is just something...different about you now."

He drew back a fraction to stare at her. Could she truly read his moods so easily? A day ago that would have concerned him, but today...today he rather liked that she could tell his feelings.

He knew she would always protect them.

He cupped her cheeks. "I am perfectly content, I promise you," he whispered. "Except that I would very much like to take you upstairs and continue this night together. If you would allow me to share your bed."

She looked at him for a long moment and then she nodded. "Yes. I would very much like that."

John smiled. Tonight was a beginning. And for the first time in a long while, he looked forward to the beginning of something good.

CHAPTER 11

John staggered into the foyer of his London home and smiled. He hadn't spent a night away from this place in years. He always made it a point not to join a woman in her bed for more than a few hours. But waking up to Mariah beside him, being able to make love to her in the sparkling light of dawn and then sharing breakfast with her…he realized he had been missing out on something very special.

But perhaps it would not have been so special with any other woman. He certainly couldn't picture doing the same with anyone but Mariah. Which was why he intended to ask her tonight if she would allow him to be her protector.

A thrill worked through him at the very thought of something more permanent with her.

A thrill that faded as his butler approached. Swanson's normally calm, unflappable countenance was pale and his lips thin.

John stared. "What is it?" he asked, his voice barely carrying. "I—did someone die? Is someone hurt?"

The butler swallowed and shook his head, sending relief through John, albeit briefly.

"No, sir," he said. "But…but your father is here, sir. He insisted on being taken to your parlor and presented with brandy while he waited."

John stepped back until he hit the door. Luckily it was shut, or he might have deposited himself down his stone steps onto his head.

"My father?" he said.

This was the second time in as many days that his estranged family had intruded upon his home. With Adam, it was a welcome intrusion after the first bit of awkwardness. But if Vaughn Rycroft was here…well, there was not going to be anything pleasant about the rest of the day.

The servant nodded. "Yes, sir. I *did* try to impress upon him that you were not in residence, nor did I have an estimated time for your return, but he refused to depart."

John shook his head to clear the shock and dismay that gripped him just as it had all throughout his childhood. He couldn't be emotional when he saw his father. He couldn't afford that. He had to collect himself or he would be bait for a very dangerous predator.

"You could not have done anything to stop him, short of physically restraining him," John reassured the servant as he worked to calm his breathing and slow his racing heart. "And even then, it might not have ended well. Do not trouble yourself. I expected his arrival, though perhaps not today. There is no use in trying to put it off."

Swanson nodded, but there was a flicker of pity in his otherwise unreadable expression. "Is there anything you require? Shall I bring you anything?"

John shook his head. "No. I don't want the bastard to have anything more than what he's already taking. But…" He hesitated and locked eyes with the servant. "In half an hour, knock and interrupt us. Remind me of an appointment. I refuse to give the man any more time than that."

"Yes, sir." Swanson straightened his shoulders. "And I shall alert

Thomason and a few of the other servants just in case the physical force you mentioned is necessary to remove him."

John smiled and patted the butler's arm. "We shall hope for the best, but you are right to prepare for the worst. Vaughn Rycroft almost always delivers it."

He turned away from the butler and toward the door to the parlor. With a deep breath, he opened it and entered the room.

His father was standing at the window, staring out on the street with his eyes narrowed. John took a moment to stare at him. He had always hated how much he looked like his father, with the same dark hair and eyes. He wanted to look like anyone else in the world, perhaps to be able to convince himself that anyone else in the world was his father.

But there was no denying a connection when Vaughn looked at him. His father was an older version of the same thing he saw in the mirror every day.

"About time you rolled in," his father hissed as he stepped toward him. It took everything in John not to step backward an equal distance.

"I didn't know I was under your curfew, *Mr. Rycroft,*" John said, emphasizing the address he chose to use. "Since I am far above the age of majority and have not spoken to you in too many years to count."

His father smirked. "You may be above the age of majority, boy, but that doesn't mean you don't need to be put in line now and then. You don't think I've watched you all these years?"

John folded his arms. "I'm certain you have. It has always been your style to spy and intrude where you were not welcome."

His father's lips pursed in displeasure and he glared at John. "Welcome or not, I am here. We have a great deal to talk about, a fact I think you know."

John shrugged. "And why would I know that? Why would that be true at all?"

His father moved forward, aggression in every line of his body.

As a boy, that look had terrified John. It almost always meant emotional or physical punishment for unseen and uncommitted crimes. Often both. His father's rage had caused him nightmares, cold sweats, terror that shook him all the way to his bones.

As a man, the same warning signs put him on guard and made his stomach clench, but John was happy to have put the fear away.

"Don't play stupid, John. I *know* your brother made an appearance here yesterday."

John shifted. The spies were hard at work, indeed.

"I suppose he did," he said quietly. "Though I'm not certain how that visit is any of your business."

Vaughn laughed, but it was anything but a pleasant sound. "I'm sure it had everything to do with the fact that I recently cut your brother off entirely and told him directly that I was turning over the inheritance of my fortune to you. No doubt he came here sniveling for a handout. So I think it has *everything* to do with me."

John shut his eyes briefly. How he wished he could block his father from his world entirely. How he wished he could pretend he had no father. But it was impossible.

"Adam mentioned something to that effect, yes. But he didn't ask for a handout at all. Just delivered a welcomed warning."

"No doubt he *warned* you of a great deal." His father leaned back with a satisfied smile. "It must have stuck in that boy's craw to tell you my fortune was being torn from him. It must have made him sick."

John stared. For years, his father had pitted the brothers against each other. As children, they had each played into his game in order to avoid the ugly, painful consequences of defying Vaughn Rycroft. As adults, their separation had only grown.

John imagined other parents might have mourned the distance between their children. Or even worked to close it.

Their father *smiled* over it.

Hatred bubbled inside of John, but he kept it in check. "The entire situation makes both of us sick, I assure you, sir."

His father laughed again and sarcasm dripped from his tone as he continued, "Oh yes, I'm certain the idea of inheriting a fortune worth well over one hundred thousand pounds and growing every day is pure devastation to you. And taking it from your brother gives you no pleasure at all. Winning is, after all, such a burden."

"Is that what you think this is?" John asked, truly surprised. "*Winning*? You don't seem to understand that I don't care about your land and your businesses and your money. Your hundred thousand pounds worth of assets is garbage to me. I do not desire it and I will not accept it. You waste your time and mine by coming here."

His father moved on him with such swiftness that John hardly had time to react before Vaughn was standing just a foot in front of him, his dark eyes flashing with rage and his fists clenched at his sides.

"Bollocks," he snapped, his tone tense with anger and violence. "You don't get to choose, John."

He shrugged and now a smile of his own fluttered on his lips temporarily. "Oh, but I do. You see, I have made my own fortune. I don't need yours."

His father sneered. "That little shipping business? It's worth, what, half of what I am offering you?"

John tensed. How did his father know that? His records were kept private.

"It matters little what the business is worth. It more than supports me."

"You lie if you say that you don't want more," his father snapped.

John considered that. Once that might have been true. Once he might have been his father's son. Not anymore.

"I lie about a great many things," he said with a dismissive wave of his hand. "But not this. I will not come under your thumb, Mr. Rycroft. So forget whatever nefarious plans you have."

His father stared at him for a moment in disbelief. "I could destroy you. And then you will have no choice."

John held his tongue. All his life his father had torn down in order to control. His toys, and even his bones, had been broken. His friends had been taken from him, his mother had been sent away to die alone because Vaughn Rycroft knew that destruction was the best way to keep his sons trapped beneath his heel.

Everything was different now. John's shipping business had been successful for years. His father's influence could perhaps take away a few of his clients, but not all. He might be damaged, but not broken.

Not ever again.

"*Try*," John said softly. "Try to destroy me."

Vaughn blinked in what could only be described as disbelief and John's heart swelled. Oh yes, his father could do nothing to him now.

Vaughn stepped away. "So you think your business is safe. I disagree, but very well. The fact that you are considering adding your brother to your payroll tells me you have no ability to make good decisions."

John moved forward. "And what do you know of that?"

Hell, he had only told his brother of his intentions to bring him aboard yesterday. His solicitor had taken over the arrangements and John trusted him completely. But his father knew. Which meant he had connections somewhere within John's business.

His father smiled over his shoulder as he turned away. "Oh, I know a great deal. A fact I hope you won't soon forget. I know how much you pay your servants. I know the club where you fence. I know you have been fucking your best friend's whore, not just once, but for quite a while now."

Now John clenched his fists. "Don't talk to me about Mariah."

His father spun around and his grin widened. "Ah, *there's* that soft spot. I knew I'd find it eventually. Interesting that this time it's nothing more than a lightskirt masquerading as something more refined. But if you pretend you don't care about what I can do to your life, perhaps you might care about what I could do to hers."

John surged forward, all his attempts at control disappearing in a flash of anger and rage so powerful he feared he might not be able to control it. That he might do what he'd fantasized about for years and kill his father where he stood.

But that would only end in ruination. Scandal. Despair.

He grabbed his father's collar and slammed him against the wall next to the window as hard as he could.

"Stay the fuck away from Mariah," he growled, low and dangerous as he held his father's gaze. Vaughn Rycroft's eyes were so dead and empty that it was sickening.

His father remained curiously silent as John released him and stepped back, trying to regain control of his breath, his heart. But soon Vaughn smiled, ugly, glee-filled and so sinister that it brought back a new passel of awful memories.

John squeezed his eyes shut. That was it. His father knew exactly what his weakness was thanks to his emotional responses. And now any dream he had briefly had of a longer future with Mariah slipped from his fingers. She could never be his. Not for more than a few days or weeks. Not if he wanted to keep her safe.

Behind them, the door to the parlor opened and Swanson stepped inside. John could see by the way his servant's shoulders were thrown back that the butler was spoiling for a fight. He couldn't help a smile at that fact, even though his body and heart ached.

"Mr. Rycroft, the meeting you are meant to attend starts in a few minutes. Should I have your carriage brought around?"

Vaughn Rycroft looked at him with a small tilt of his head. "I should go," he said. "It seems we're finished here."

John looked at his father. What had been done could not be undone now. All he could do was try to find the best way to prevent anything worse in the future.

"Yes," he said softly. "You and I are finished."

His father smirked as he headed for the door. "We'll see, boy. We'll see."

Then he was gone, with Swanson trailing after him, likely to ensure he stole nothing on the way out. John appreciated the gesture, but in truth, there was no point to it. His father might not take the silver, but he had already stolen something of far greater value.

A future he hadn't even known he desired so deeply.

CHAPTER 12

When Mariah had been invited to supper at John's home, to be followed by a night at the opera, she was delighted. Their most recent encounter, the night they spent together, had brought them closer than ever. And even though she had strenuously denied that fact to Vivien, Mariah welcomed the new closeness. She wanted to spend more time with John, to make love to him and to engage in conversation and connection. She had never experienced anything like it before and she reveled in it.

But now, sitting at his table, with him far down the length of it staring at food he was not eating, her delight faded to be replaced with concern and frustration. It seemed every time they took a step forward, he dug in his heels and forced them two steps back.

Which begged the question, if he was so resistant to any kind of connection to her, why did he continue to see her? Why not let her go entirely and simply move on? If he did so, she could return to her search for a protector, and he could go back to the meaningless encounters he had enjoyed for so long.

It seemed very unfair. And yet she couldn't be angry. Not when his mouth was so drawn down and his shoulders so tense.

"John, you have not spoken more than five words the entire

night," she finally said, setting her fork aside. "Clearly, I have done something to offend you. Tell me what it is now and let us deal with it."

He blinked and stared at her blankly. "You, offend me?" he said softly. "No. I'm sorry, Mariah, if that is the impression I have given you. You have caused me no offense, I assure you."

She shoved back and stood from the ridiculously long table that had been designed for twenty people at least. Tossing her napkin aside, she stalked to the end where he sat and took the chair immediately at his right. He watched her every move with an unreadable expression that was as maddening as everything else.

She took his hand and held it gently.

"Then what is it, John? You have been distant and unhappy since my arrival," she said softly. "If that has not been caused by me, then what has put this wall between us?"

He stared at her with an expression she had never seen before and she thought, just for a moment, that he might let her in. Her heart leapt at the thought and she leaned in to encourage openness from him. But instead he slid his hand from hers and sat back in his chair, as aloof as ever.

"Mariah, I would like to employ a guard for you."

She rocked back in surprise. He could not have said anything else to shock her more.

"What?" she asked, unable to form any more coherent or eloquent reply to the madness he presented to her.

His frown deepened. "A guard. He would not intrude upon you, I assure you. Simply trail you to and from your appointments and sit outside them. He would also keep watch over your home."

Mariah blinked and briefly wondered if what she was experiencing was a dream. After all, this conversation was as nonsensical as any she'd ever had in her sleep with butterflies or cats. But she could not imagine a dream involving John that would be so serious, so she had to be awake, after all.

"I do understand what you mean by a guard," she said slowly.

"And my reaction is not based upon how much I fear such a person would intrude upon my daily activities. It is based upon the fact that I have no idea why you think I would need or even *want* such a thing!"

John hesitated and there was a mere glimmer of emotion in his eyes that caught Mariah off guard. It was *fear*. But of course he swept it away with one blink and shrugged.

"Owen's death was very public. The world knows you are living in your home alone, and perhaps with a more limited staff, yes?" he asked, his tone calm and collected, as if there were no emotion to this conversation.

Mariah flinched. She *had* let two footmen go today in an effort to make her purse leaner and buy herself a little more time. Of course she was spending that time with John, not looking for a new protector who could save her from her dire situation.

"Yes," she said softly.

He shrugged. "Then you see, I simply do not wish for anyone to take advantage of you."

She shook her head. "That is pure bollocks, John. I don't believe you for a moment. There is more to this 'suggestion' than that. You do not hire a guard for nameless fears that have in no way manifested themselves, you hire a few large footmen and talk to my driver. This is about something more."

He drew back in a moment of surprise and then tossed his napkin aside. "Think what you will then, Mariah. The man has already been spoken to and will arrive at your home tomorrow."

Mariah let out her breath in a shocked huff. "If you have already made these arrangements on my behalf, why bother asking my leave at all?"

"I did not ask. I was simply being polite in informing you," he replied with a shrug.

Anger swelled in her. "Oh yes, you are the picture of politeness, John."

He pursed his lips, but gave no other response to her outrage.

"Now, are you ready to depart?" he asked, as if they had been discussing nothing more important than the weather or the price of fabric for a new gown.

She stared at him. "You must be in jest. Do you think I would wish to go out when you have hardly spoken to me all night except to demand I accept a guard for a threat you lie about?" She shook her head. "No. I do not wish to spend an evening with you. I am going home."

His fingers curled into a fist on the tabletop and it was through clenched teeth that he said, "No."

Her eyes went wide, even though she wished she could stay as stoic as he managed to do. "No?"

He shook his head. "If you don't want to go to the opera, we will stay in, but you're not leaving."

She slammed a hand on the table. "Oh, you do vex me endlessly! How *dare* you claim you have a right to dictate my actions? What happened to my carefree friend who was to take me as a temporary lover?"

His lips pursed and for a moment she saw she had hit a mark with him. She should have felt triumphant that she had, but she didn't. Only confused and exhausted by his sudden overbearing protectiveness.

"I—I am truly sorry, Mariah," he said, his voice low and filled with true regret. But that was gone when he said, "But I must insist."

She straightened her spine. "As do I. Good night, John."

She turned toward the door, but the screech of his chair and the steel of his fingers closing around her wrist let her know it wasn't going to be that easy. She spun back toward him to protest his bullying, but he didn't allow her to speak. He dragged her against him and then his mouth was on hers, hard and demanding, hot and heavy with desire and promise.

She wanted to fight him, to refuse him, but as his tongue molded to hers, she lost all ability to say no, to pull away, to do anything but arch against his chest and moan out pleasure against his lips. She felt him smile as he spun her around, pressing her to the edge of the table and stroking her with his hips.

The steel of his erection was evident even through all the layers of their clothes and her treacherous body ignored her outrage and instead ripened and readied for his invasion. Her nipples rasped against the silk of her chemise and telltale wetness pooled between her legs and heightened the throbbing of her clitoris.

"I...don't...want...this," she tried weakly between passionate kisses.

He drew back a fraction and stared down at her, his eyes lit by passion. "I sincerely doubt that, since you are rubbing your hips against me in a most pleasing rhythm."

She blushed as she realized he was correct, she *was* rubbing against him with the same fervor as she would once they were naked together.

"But if you are not in jest, say it again and I will stop." He lifted a hand to her breast and cupped it, rubbing his thumb against her nipple in a slow circle. "If you have enough breath to speak, that is."

She squeezed her eyes shut, trying to ignore the sharp bursts of pleasure that radiated from his circling thumb, warming her limbs, creating flutters in her belly and bringing her closer, inch by inch, to orgasm.

She let out her breath in a cry and he chuckled. "Should I take that as a yes?"

He plucked her nipple again and she jolted. "Yes!" she screamed and he crushed his mouth to hers again.

She tore at his jacket, surrendering to the fact that she had no defense against him, even if she wanted one. Her need for him was the most powerful force she had ever encountered. She had no strength to deny it, to reject it. And he knew it and could exploit that fact.

He lifted her onto the table and opened her legs to step between them. She moaned as the dishes behind her clattered. Without preamble, he reached back to sweep them out of the way. She heard a cup crash to the floor and silverware bounce under the table, but she didn't care. Nor did he, judging by the fact that he shoved at her skirts, lifting them up around her waist before he took the seat she had abandoned and dragged it to the table.

"A feast," he all but purred. "How can I resist?"

He pressed his lips to her slick entrance and began to lick her in earnest, hard strokes. She gasped as she clung to the edge of the wood and lifted herself against him to meet his stokes. He spread her sex open with his fingers and lapped at her juices just like they were indeed a dessert to be savored. He didn't seem to care that they were in the dining room or that the servants had not been ordered to stay out. He didn't seem to care about anything except thoroughly devouring her every slick and ready fold.

"John," she gasped as sensation mobbed her, overwhelmed her. It was too intense, too focused, too much in every sense.

He grinned up at her and then pressed two fingers to her entrance, gliding them deep within her clenching body as he returned his tongue to her aching, hard clitoris. He sucked the little nub of nerves between his lips and swirled his tongue around and around, flicking her with his teeth and tormenting her in every way imaginable.

The orgasm started slow, a few little twitches and vibrations, but as if he sensed her crisis, he increased both the speed of his thrusting fingers and the suction of his mouth on her sex. She cried out in utter release, writhing on the table, her heels digging into the edge as she lifted her hips helplessly.

But he allowed her no respite. As she reached the height of her orgasm, he withdrew his wet fingers from her sex and touched her backside. Using her own juices to lubricate the tender opening, he slid them inside her forbidden passage gently.

Mariah's eyes flew open in surprise and pleasure at this new invasion and her orgasm intensified yet again as he licked her sex and pumped his fingers into her backside with slow, steady pressure. She was full and hot and unable to control her reactions, her screams, her wildly slamming hips as wave after wave of unfettered pleasure mobbed her and made her weak.

"Still want to leave?" he asked, removing his mouth from her sex and his fingers from her backside.

He looked up at her from between her thighs, his eyes dark with desire and bright with promises of things to come, and she could do nothing but shake her head.

"You know you make me too weak to refuse you," she said, an accusation softened by the fact that she was still panting with release.

He smiled, so wicked, so sensual, and she shivered as she realized he wasn't even close to being finished with her. Her release was not enough, he wanted more…more…always more.

He reached up and stripped his shirt off in a few smooth movements. His trousers quickly followed and he stood before her, naked in the bright lights of the dining hall. She stared in continued awe at his beauty as her mouth began to water with desire.

"The servants—" she began, but her voice held no strength in its one attempt at refusal.

"Let them watch," he growled as he lowered himself over her on the table.

His mouth moved over hers and she tasted the earthy, sweet flavor of her own body on his lips. She arched with a moan both at the taste and the way it had come to be there. He smiled against her mouth.

"Delicious, isn't it?" he murmured between long, languid kisses. "Better than any dessert my servants would bring to us. And so is this."

He positioned himself at her entrance and stroked deep within her, filling her entirely with just the flex of his hips. She cried out against his mouth, digging her nails into his bare shoulders. He hissed out a breath as she clung to him and then he began to move.

No, move was not a descriptive enough term for what he did.

They had made love many times before. It had been sweet and

gentle, it had been dark and passionate, but this…this was something else. As Mariah looked up at him, he seemed to transform from controlled gentleman to wild creature, driven to take her, to claim her, to fill her and to suck every bit of pleasure from her.

He pounded hard, rotating his hips to hit her clitoris with every stroke, lifting her backside more firmly as he took and took with ever increasing desire.

But it didn't seem to be enough. Not for him. With a grunt of frustration, he withdrew from her aching body and stared down at her, panting, his cock hard and wet against his belly.

"Stand up," he ordered. "And take off your dress."

Mariah didn't even think of refusing. She might still be angry and frustrated by a great many things in this strange relationship they had developed, but the passion between them was not one of them. It was too powerful to resist, even if she had wanted to do so, which she decidedly did not.

She got to her feet, clutching at the table to maintain her balance on shaky legs and then quickly stripped open the buttons along the front of her gown. As she stepped from the dress, she couldn't help but notice the wrinkled destruction their lovemaking had already wrought. And there was some kind of stain on the fabric that might not ever come out.

She didn't care. As she stood naked before him, she would not have been troubled if he went to her closet and burned every pretty gown she owned. As long as he took her, fulfilled her, after he did so. Clothing was highly overrated.

"Turn around," he said, his voice gravelly and low as he stared at her with unwavering focus and intensity.

She smiled as she realized what he was going to do. But while she liked that he took the control, she wasn't about to give it all to him entirely. She slowly turned around, taking her time to place each palm on the edge of the table, spreading her legs to reveal her sex for him. Then she peeked over her shoulder, blinking in what she hoped was the image of pure wickedness.

"You mean like this?" she asked, innocent as a lamb in her tone even as she displayed herself so wantonly.

He didn't answer, at least not with words. He rushed her, reaching around to cup her breasts as he pushed his cock deep within her. From behind, she felt all the sensations so differently, so much more intensely, and almost immediately the orgasm he had created with his mouth returned and crashed over her again.

He drove her through it, pounding hard into her as he thumbed her nipples and circled his hips to stoke every part of her sex. She scratched her nails against the table, trying to get a grip on something, *anything* to keep her steady, to keep her from losing herself entirely.

But it was impossible. Her vision blurred as her crisis reached its peak and only John kept her upright as he roared out a loud, animal cry of pleasure and spent deep within her twitching, clenching body.

Mariah draped herself over the table, weak with pleasure as he withdrew from her body. Slowly, she rolled over and stared up at the ceiling high above. A fork was jabbing her hip and she was fairly certain that most of the plates once on the table were now shattered on the floor below them, but for the moment it didn't matter as John wrapped his arms around her and gathered her to his chest. Together, they sank to the floor next to the dining room table.

She feared nothing, she felt nothing except for the warmth of his weight pressed against her. In that moment, everything was perfect.

But deep within her was a nagging sensation that perfect couldn't last. After all, it never had before.

CHAPTER 13

Mariah poured Vivien a cup of tea before she settled into a comfortable chair in her parlor. She smiled at her friend, though the expression was entirely forced. She felt anything but the comfort and ease that the look implied.

A fact which Vivien recognized immediately. She arched an elegant brow before she spoke.

"My dear, you have been grinding your teeth since the moment I arrived. What has you so frustrated?"

Mariah folded her hands in her lap and let out a long sigh. "Did you see the man seated on horseback across from my home?"

Vivien blinked before she shook her head in the negative. Mariah shut her eyes, counted to ten so that she would not reveal her tangled emotions and motioned to the window. The two women approached it together and Mariah pulled back the shade to reveal the busy street below. There, seated on his horse, staring at her home, was a tall, muscular gentleman dressed in fine livery.

Vivien drew back and looked at Mariah in question. "I suppose I *did* notice him now that you point him out. How odd to see someone just sitting in the street like that. Why is he there? Who is he?"

"A guard," Mariah said as she returned to her seat and flopped down with a huff of breath. "Courtesy of Mr. John Rycroft."

Vivien followed her and perched on the very edge of her own seat. Her face was ashen with sudden worry. "A guard? Whatever for?"

"He refuses to tell me," Mariah said with a groan.

Vivien shook her head. "Were you threatened? Is there some kind of indication that Owen's death was not the accident we presumed it to be?"

Mariah shivered at that idea. "*No!* None of those things, at least as far as I know. John simply told me one night that I was to have a guard. Then he pretended as if life were normal and refused to give me any more information."

"How very odd," Vivien muttered.

Mariah nodded emphatically. "Odd is certainly one word for it, though I have a few less kind ones for his behavior. He insists upon running my life, and I suppose I could accept that if he were my protector. But he is not. He refuses to offer me that benefit."

Vivien tapped a finger against her lip, thinking. "I've never heard of him involving himself so deeply in a lover's life. It is so unlike him."

Mariah nodded. "Indeed, it is. Especially since we agreed at the beginning of this arrangement that it would only be a light and amusing diversion for us both. Now I somehow have a sentinel at my door. I'm surprised he hasn't set wolves to patrol my back gate. Or arranged to have the Queen's guard pace along my rooftop."

Vivien tilted her head and Mariah felt her friend judging and analyzing her. "You pretend to be angry, but I do not sense that in you when you speak."

Mariah's mouth dropped open in surprise and outrage. "Of course I am angry! John Rycroft's overbearing brutishness is not to be endured."

Vivien raised both eyebrows as if she knew there was more. Of course, she *did* know. Vivien never missed anything, nor let it go if she saw it. Which was why there was no point in denying it.

Mariah shifted. "And I cannot deny that I am also worried by how intense our bond has become. There is so much at play here that I do not understand. He will not *allow* me to understand. There is the relationship with his family, his refusal to let anyone close to him—"

Vivien gave her a look like she was daft. "The fact that he seems to believe there is a *threat* against you."

Mariah pursed her lips. "Yes, of course there is that."

Vivien nodded and dropped her gaze away. She took a long sip of tea and then locked eyes with Mariah. "I think you should obtain a new protector."

Mariah's breath left her lungs in a whoosh. "I—I am trying to do so, Vivien! You know this."

Vivien looked less than convinced. "Are you? It is a half-hearted effort at best, my dear."

Her words cut off any denials Mariah might have had on her lips. With her friend she could be, nay she *had* to be, perfectly honest. Even if she hadn't been so very candid with herself, lately.

"I—" she began, then shook her head as heat flooded her cheeks. How humiliating to have to broach this subject with her friend. "Yes, I admit, you are right that I haven't tried as hard as I should be to find a new man to take the place Owen left empty. I think perhaps I was not as ready to do so as I thought when I began."

Vivien shook her head. "Oh, I don't think your readiness or willingness to be with another man is in question. I fear it is the opposite, entirely."

"I don't understand what you could possibly mean," Mariah said.

She was beginning to feel a little peevish about the entire situation. John told her what to do, Vivien told her about her own feelings. Could she do nothing for herself?

Vivien's next words ceased her annoyance entirely. "I fear you are developing feelings for John Rycroft."

Mariah jumped to her feet, her breath ripped from her lungs. Her mind spun as she tried to find words for a contradiction of that statement.

"No," she finally gasped. "That is ridiculous, of course! John and I are friends, that is the only emotional attachment we share. Our current physical arrangement is entirely separate from any matters of the heart."

"Oh dear God," Vivien muttered as she raised a hand to stop Mariah from continuing her denials. "Don't try to delude me as ferociously as you attempt to delude yourself. It is exhausting for me to hear and I'm sure it is equally so for you to say. You care for him."

Mariah opened her mouth then snapped it shut. "I will concede that I do care for him, though I go no further than that in my confessions."

Vivien shook her head with an indulgent smile. "Very well, we shall not argue that topic any further. But I must still make my point."

"And that is?" Mariah asked weakly. In truth, she wasn't certain she was ready for Vivien's grand argument on her life and her heart.

"He will not…" Vivien paused, looked troubled. "Or perhaps he *cannot* give you what you require to secure your future. And in this instance, it could be better, nay imperative, to be selfish and protect yourself."

Mariah hesitated. Every word Vivien said was perfectly reasonable, and she certainly respected her friend for her success as a mistress. But she also couldn't deny the ripping tug those words created in her heart.

She paced to the window, hoping that Vivien wouldn't see too deeply into her soul if she could not stare her down.

"You are saying, I suppose, that I must turn away from John now in order to shield myself."

Vivien was quiet and her silence forced Mariah to look at her. She saw pity in her friend. Pity she despised. Vivien nodded once.

Mariah nodded. "I realize you are utterly correct when I am able to consider your thoughts logically."

"Logic is hard to come by in matters of the heart," Vivien said, her voice so soft it barely carried. "I know."

"Do you?" Mariah laughed, though she found no humor in the discussion. "You always seem so reasonable. I cannot imagine you've ever been so foolish as to be swept away."

Vivien's expression wavered for a brief moment and Mariah was certain she saw a flash of pain on her friend's face. But then it was gone.

"I am pleased you hold such a high opinion of me," Vivien said. "Since you do, may I offer to be your voice of wisdom?"

Mariah didn't answer for a moment, mostly because she knew the "wisdom" Vivien was about to impart would likely tear her from John.

"I know you told me once you did not wish to be matched," Vivien said, without waiting for Mariah to accept her offer of advice. "But I cannot help what my nature is. I have recently become aware of a gentleman who is looking for a new mistress. I believe he might be a good fit for you, both in temperament and in his ability and *willingness* to take care of you."

Mariah squeezed her eyes shut to ward off the pain that suddenly mobbed her.

"But John—" she whispered.

Vivien leapt to her feet and crossed the room. She caught Mariah's hands and held them tightly. "John told you to continue your search. And has given you *no* reason to stop."

Mariah could not deny those facts, so she nodded.

Vivien's voice gentled. "Please. Meet me at my home tonight."

Mariah glanced over her shoulder. "And what about him?"

She motioned toward the guard and Vivien pursed her lips. "We will find a way to slip away from him. You will certainly be safe where I will take you, you don't need John's governess watching over you. He will only make you nervous and remind you of…of things better left forgotten."

Mariah sighed. There was a reason she could think of no argument to this plan—there was none. Vivien was right on every count, and her own hesitation came from foolish flutters of her heart, not solid reasons for refusal.

She pushed everything else away and nodded. "Yes. I will go with you. It is the best thing for me."

Vivien wrapped an arm around her and led her back to the chairs to finish their tea. "My dear, I know this sort of thing feels like bad medicine right now in the heat of this moment, but once it is over and resolved, I think you will be happy you took my advice."

Mariah nodded, but she felt anything but positive about her upcoming evening. Vivien was right. This was very bad medicine, indeed…but she would take her bitter pill and pray it would cure her of the continuing desire she felt for John. Before the desire broke her permanently.

~

John leaned over the ledger, paying close attention to the marks his brother was making on this copy. Adam had always been good with numbers and was proving to be an interesting addition to his business.

His brother took a long look at the line of figures before him, then set his quill aside.

"You truly are a self-made man," he said in unguarded wonder that made John's chest swell with pride. Pride that faded when his brother continued, "It makes me feel very weak indeed for ever relying on our father for my purse."

John frowned as he took a seat across from his brother at his desk. "A sentiment I'm sure that bastard would love to hear." He shook his head. "Don't say it out loud or ever feel it and give him the satisfaction."

His thoughts wandered to their father, so smug and assured in his ability to control, to win any war. He would almost admire that quality if Vaughn Rycroft didn't use his confidence to crush and maim on a regular basis. Hatred swelled in him as their last conversation replayed in his mind.

His brother shifted. "Am I to assume he did come to you, then?"

John shook off his memories and his strong reactions to them and nodded. "Of course. We both knew he would, but I thank you for your warning regardless. I was, at least, somewhat prepared. Though he is far worse than I remembered. A great feat, I assure you."

Adam ran a hand over his face, but there was no covering the pain his brother felt. "He does not improve with age, no," he said quietly. "How could he threaten you, though? With me, it was money that gave him power. That is not the case here, obviously."

John shoved to his feet. "He tried money, of course, but quickly recognize that tactic would get him nowhere. So he turned to more personal warfare. He threatened those I care about. You and..." He trailed off. "...and others."

Adam tilted his head and there was no denying the curiosity on his face. "Others?"

John waved him off. There was no way he was going to say Mariah's name out loud and admit to his brother, himself or anyone else that he cared for her.

"It is unimportant."

But that was hardly the case. Thoughts of Mariah had recently clouded his mind more and more. Both in worries of what his father might do to trouble her...and of more pleasant thoughts of the bond that was steadily growing between them, despite his every attempt to bring it to an end.

Adam shrugged. "I can take care of myself, so if his threats against me are of worry to you, please don't trouble yourself." He hesitated. "But, brother, do not underestimate our father. He can be...ruthless."

John barked out an empty laugh. "He always was."

Adam shifted. "Yes, but more so now. He will not stop until he has what he wants."

John wrinkled his brow and focused more firmly on his brother. There seemed to be some subtext to his words that John did not fully comprehend. Adam was far too worried for a normal response to their father's intrusion.

"Adam, what is it that you fear?" he asked softly.

His brother returned his gaze to the ledger before him and shrugged. "I could not say, exactly. But I certainly hope you will not allow yourself, or these others you refuse to reveal, to fall prey to him."

John clenched his fists. There *was* more to his brother's response than Adam was saying and he wished to pry out the details. But their reunion was still so fresh that he feared pushing would only drive his brother away.

He had a guard on Mariah now, and never had he been so firmly certain of a decision. She would be safe. He would settle for nothing less.

"There will be no prey for our father to find, Adam," he said as he settled into his seat. "I will be sure of that."

CHAPTER 14

Vivien held Mariah's hand as they slipped out the servants' entrance of her estate. It was dark behind the house, but a footman holding a small lantern led the way down a path into an alleyway where a carriage was parked. Mariah smiled. Vivien's regular vehicle was only the best and highly recognizable with its bright red trim.

This carriage was not. It was small, a bit run-down and would blend in perfectly with a thousand others rumbling around on the streets this night.

"Where did you find this thing?" she asked.

Vivien did not reply as the footman helped them up into the rig and shut the squeaky door behind them. Inside, the carriage was perfectly serviceable, though nothing fancy.

"This was a vehicle I was provided many years ago by my first protector," she finally explained. "I kept it even when I had newer models, both as a reminder of where I began and a conveyance for my servants if they needed to go somewhere. I would hate to have them being forced to use hacks, which are very expensive."

The vehicle jolted into motion and as Mariah reached out to steady herself on the wall of the carriage, she smiled at her friend.

"You really are the kindest of mistresses to your servants, aren't you?"

Vivien shrugged. "I try to treat anyone in my employ with care. After all, they not only see things that could be very incriminating, but they are also hardly beneath me. I am, after all, a servant in my own way. Or I have been in the past."

"Now you are a self-made woman," Mariah laughed, "who all other courtesans and mistresses wish to imitate."

To her surprise, Vivien did not answer that compliment, but turned to look out the window. In the dim light from the street lamps outside, she saw her friend's face lift in a smile.

"We are about to pass your guard. Let us see if we have fooled him."

Mariah leaned forward to peer out of the window Vivien indicated. Sure enough, they were approaching the man on horseback. As their carriage rolled past, she shrank back against the seat, even as she stared. The man shifted on his horse slightly, but there was no other reaction. And as she leaned to see his figure disappear behind them, he made no motion to make chase.

She flopped back against the carriage seat with a sigh of relief, although there was more anxiety twisting her stomach in knots than pleasure.

"John will be furious when he finds out what we've done," she said softly.

Vivien turned away from the window and there was a look of concern on her friend's face as she stared. "That may be true, *if* he finds out."

"You don't think he will?"

Vivien shrugged. "We will be back at a reasonable hour, I'm sure. There would be no reason for him to think anything other than that you and I shared a long supper. Unless you tell him otherwise."

Mariah shifted. Her friend was right, of course. And she had no intention of telling John that she had snuck away to meet with a potential protector, not unless that new relationship worked in her favor. But the idea of withholding the truth, perhaps even lying outright to him, did not sit well.

Vivien sighed. "My dear, it is best if you don't think of John tonight."

Mariah returned her attention to the sights out the window. Vivien was right, of course, but if one thing had become clear in her life over the past few days, if was that it was impossible for her not to think of John. He was a constant figure in her mind, in her dreams. She woke with his name on her lips and went to sleep with his face in her mind.

And all this had led her to one terrifying conclusion, one fact that had peeked into her mind thanks to her earlier conversation with Vivien and taken root there, until now it was an undeniable force. One she had denied in the afternoon, but could no longer do so.

"I...I am in love with him," she whispered.

She sucked in a breath. Now that it had been said out loud, she realized how true that statement was. She loved John Rycroft. Worse, she had loved him for some time. Oh, she had said they were friends, she had told herself that the bond that seemed to have existed between them from the moment they met was only affection caused by their mutual feelings for Owen.

But it wasn't true. There had been something more between them from the start.

Vivien had remained silent as all these tangled thoughts raced through Mariah's mind, but now she whispered, "I know that, my dear. I know you love him."

Mariah sighed. Of course she did. Vivien knew everything. And what she must think of her now!

"You know," she said, hoping to find a way to explain herself. "I have thought a great deal about Owen since his death last month. I believed that I was in love with *him*. And I did care for him. Deeply. But this is...different."

To her surprise, Vivien leaned forward and seemed truly eager to hear more. "How?"

Mariah pursed her lips as she thought of the question. She had never allowed herself to analyze the differences before, only let them flit through her mind before squashing them and calling them unkind.

"With Owen, I spent a great deal of time trying to love him despite himself. Because he could be very…selfish, I had to forgive his faults, ignore his weaknesses and so very often remain silent on my opinions that might be so bold as to differ from his own. He required that of me, as a mistress."

"I admit, I did see those very things when I looked at the two of you together," Vivien said.

Mariah jerked her gaze to her friend. "You did? Why did you never say anything?"

Vivien smiled sadly. "You are unlike me in many ways. You have been a man's lover for years, but you still retain some innocence about you. You needed to believe you loved him in order to continue forward on your path. And while you two were together, what good would it have done to correct you? To ask you to face Owen's imperfections? It only would have hurt you."

Mariah shook her head. "I suppose that may be right. But I still would have appreciated your opinion. I respect it a great deal."

Vivien reached across the carriage and squeezed her hand. "Then I will give it to you now. I *do* think what you share with John is very different. You two have a strong connection, one that comes from both sides. You are a good match and that is abundantly clear whenever you are in a room together."

"Yes." Mariah cleared her throat past a sudden lump there. "But that difference can give me no more joy than my forced affections toward Owen did. John has made it abundantly clear that he cannot be with me. Or more specifically, he doesn't *want* to be with me."

"It is more the first than the second, I can almost guarantee it," Vivien said, her tone very low and filled with comfort.

Mariah appreciated the effort, but she shrugged. "One or the other, the result is the same. And so you are correct. I must put John out of my mind and find someone to protect me. As much as I would like to curl up in a ball and simply mourn what I cannot have, what I almost had, it is not possible."

"No, you cannot do that," Vivien said, her voice suddenly distant. "Women of our station do not have that luxury to mourn love. This is our life and we can do nothing but live it as it has been presented to us."

Mariah nodded. "And I intend to do so."

"Good," Vivien said and her tone was now clear and strong as ever. "My dear friend, let me say one more thing on the topic and then we shall not speak of it again unless you desire it."

"Very well."

"John Rycroft is a fool not to love you," Vivien said with a shake of her head. "And so was Owen. But a man's love is a very dangerous thing anyway, so you may not realize it, but you could have dodged a very dangerous situation."

Mariah smiled. Her friend meant well, but her words did not help. She shrugged. "I have never experienced the love you describe, so I must take your word for it."

She looked out the window and was relieved to see that they were turning into the long drive of a city estate.

"It appears we are here, wherever the mysterious *here* is," she said, her tone as bright as she could make it under the circumstances. "And I shall shine and coo and seduce to the best of my abilities."

But as Vivien laughed and they prepared to exit the carriage, Mariah knew what she said was nothing but a lie. She might pretend a great deal, but a part of her was dying tonight. A part she desperately wanted to save, even though it wasn't possible.

∾

Mariah smiled at their host from across the room and did not have to force the expression. Viscount Felix Edmondstone was a well-known and highly respected man of the *ton*. He was older than she, much older; she guessed somewhere in his late forties. He had lost his wife three years before and had never had lovers during their time together, so she hadn't met him before now, but she liked him a great deal. He seemed kind, intelligent, gentlemanly, and from the way he talked to her and kept his stare on her, he liked her well enough too.

He did nothing to stir her body or her heart, but that was best. A mistress wasn't supposed to feel strong passions or emotions. Doing so once, let alone twice, had more than proven that fact.

She turned away from the gentleman and poured herself a glass of wine from the decanter on the sideboard. As she took a sip, she felt a gentle hand on her forearm and turned to find Vivien standing at her side.

"Would you like to take a turn about the parlor down the hallway? Lord Edmondstone tells me there are some very rare books in that room and I know how you love your reading."

Mariah nodded in relief. She wasn't having a bad time, by any means, but getting away from the crowd sounded heavenly. The two women linked arms and both gave a nod to their host as they slipped from the room and down the hallway to another parlor. Once they were inside, Vivien released her and Mariah leaned back against the closed door with a sigh.

"It cannot be as terrible as your expression implies!" Vivien said.

Mariah shook her head. "Oh no, not at all. Is my face really so awful?" She found a mirror above the fireplace and examined herself. She did look a bit drawn. "I hope he did not feel the same way."

Vivien moved to the fire to look at her reflection as well. "No, it wasn't until you left the room that you relaxed into this expression of a tormented lady."

"Good." Mariah stepped away and paced to the window to stare outside. "I promise you, I am not having a dreadful time. Lord Edmondstone is everything good and gentlemanly."

"He is, indeed," Vivien agreed. "He has not had a mistress in nearly fifteen years. He gave that all up when he married his late wife. I thought he would be a good match to you, as he is not wild, he is kind and he will likely want your company as much as your body. More to the point, he is capable and willing of taking care of you if you do the same for him."

Mariah could hardly keep her frown from deepening on her face. "Yes, that is exactly what I need. He will do, I suppose."

But her thoughts flitted immediately, as they had been all night, to John and his passionate embraces. His kiss, his whispers of desire against her ear. To the connection they shared that went so much deeper than friendship.

Vivien took her hand and the act mercifully cleared her mind of those troubling thoughts.

"I agree that he could be the one for you. That is why I brought you here, but Mariah, do not jump so quickly. This is a first meeting. Have a few more, get to know the man and *then* make your decision."

Mariah shifted. Once again, Vivien's voice of reason was quite correct, but it was hard to follow. Knowing she loved John and could never have him made her want to run. And entering into a protector/mistress relationship with Edmondstone was one way to do just that. John would let her go if she found another.

Vivien released her hand. "I shall leave you alone for a moment and make your excuses. Do take a look at the rare books, for that is what I intend to tell our host and other guests that you were taken in by."

"Vivien," Mariah said as her friend moved for the door. She turned there with a questioning tilt of her head. "Thank you. Your friendship is all that makes this odd situation bearable."

Vivien's face softened. "Of course. My friendship is something you shall always be able to depend upon, no matter what happens with Edmondstone, John Rycroft or any other man."

Then her friend was gone, leaving Mariah to collect herself. Not an easy task, considering how busy her mind and how heavy her heart were. And both were filled with memories of only one person.

She sighed as she turned to examine the bookshelves Vivien had offered as a reason for her to take a moment to herself. She doubted even books could offer her respite, but at least it was worth trying.

There was a small bookshelf against the back wall between two comfortable chairs and she moved over toward it. She bent down at her waist and looked over the titles, making note of a few she found interesting so she could gush over them later for the benefit of her host.

Finally, she straightened up and turned to exit the room, but as she did so there was a flash of movement from the corner of her eye, a burst of pain as something connected squarely to the side of her head and then darkness as she slumped to the floor.

John stared at the ledger he had been examining with his brother earlier in the day. Adam had made notes in the margins here and there, corrections, as well as suggestions for savings and increasing growth. He *should* have been focused on those things, especially considering that Adam's notes were quite detailed and interesting.

But he wasn't.

All he could think about was Mariah.

"Fuck," he cursed as he shoved his chair away from his desk with violence and paced to the window. It was getting late and the lights from the streetlamps and houses glittered like diamonds all around him. He had always liked the night, been more comfortable in the shadows it provided.

But now the night reminded him of her too. How he should be

with her right now. How he had spent so many nights tangled in her body. Worse yet, how he had spent so many nights courting her smile or listening to her speak on topics that were a passion to her.

He rubbed his eyes and tried to forget, but his traitorous mind would not allow that. He was a prisoner to himself and there was no ignoring or denying that fact.

There was a light knock at his door and he spun around to face his servant in relief. An interruption would at least force him not to think of her for five minutes.

"Yes?" he asked as Swanson stepped into the doorway.

The butler, normally so composed, seemed a little rattled. "Sir… you have a delivery."

John glanced at the clock on his mantle and blinked. It was nearly midnight. "So late?" he asked.

The servant held out a bulky package, wrapped in white paper twisted around what was obviously some kind of fabric.

"Sir…" he said as John moved forward to take it. "Th-there appears to be *blood* on the outer wrapping."

He turned the package over as John rushed to him, and sure enough, there was a thick, dark fleck of red liquid on the seam of the paper. John stared.

"Could it be ink?" he asked.

Swanson shrugged. "I hope so."

"Stand by," John said. "And be prepared to send someone to fetch the Watch if need be."

Swanson nodded sharply. "I've already told one of the younger footmen to prepare himself."

John smiled despite the tension. He could always depend on his servants.

Slowly, he peeled away the paper, being careful to leave the spot of red intact in case there was an investigation in the future. Inside there was a piece of linen wound 'round something heavy, and to his horror, more of the red liquid dotted the fabric.

He and the butler exchanged a quick glance before he flipped the fabric aside and revealed what was inside. What he saw made him stagger backward, catching himself on the edge of the desk before he fell.

"What is it?" Swanson asked as he leaned closer in the light.

"It—it is a necklace Mariah sometimes wears," John choked out. "And it is splashed with blood."

CHAPTER 15

John pulled his horse up short in front of Mariah's home and was down and running before the animal even fully stopped. He pounded on the door with his fist, even as he tested it. It was locked, of course. As he waited for a servant to arrive, he looked around.

The guard he had hired to track Mariah and protect her was nowhere to be found. Which meant either he had been incapacitated...or she wasn't here.

The door cracked to reveal Mariah's butler Lymon, his eyes wide and his face pale thanks to the racket John had been making. The man was even wielding a heavy candlestick up almost as if it was a weapon, but when he saw it was John outside, he lowered it with a blinking stare of surprise.

"Mr. Rycroft?" he asked. "I—we did not expect you this evening."

"Where is Mariah?" John demanded as he shoved past the butler into her foyer. The house was strangely quiet. Too quiet, and John's desperation mounted. "Mariah! Mar—"

"Sir, she is not here," Lymon interrupted with irritation, but his tone and his face had begun to reflect a deep worry which mirrored John's own.

His heart sank. "Where is she?"

Lymon tilted his head. "I don't know all her plans, of course, but she did say she was going to Miss Manning's home for the evening, just as she has done many times before. A fact you know as well as I do. What is it, sir? What is going on?"

John bit his lip. "Miss Mariah may be in danger, Lymon."

The butler's eyes went wide. "Danger?"

John nodded as nausea rolled up on him. He tried not to think of all the possibilities of how someone would get her necklace, covered in what appeared to be blood, but images still creeped in. Of Mariah in an alleyway somewhere. Of her injured, in pain and frightened. Of her dead.

He shook the thoughts away with a moan of pain he couldn't suppress. "Are you certain she went to Vivien's?"

The servant nodded. "Yes. She was dressed in a pretty evening gown and told me she would be back late in the evening. I assumed there was a party."

John pursed his lips. Vivien's parties were notorious. And he was almost always invited to them. Or knew about them, at any rate. There had been *no* gathering planned at her home tonight.

"Did Mariah say anything to let you know where they might be going for this soiree?"

Lymon drew back in affront that was not pretended. "She doesn't share those facts with me, sir. I wouldn't dare intrude upon her privacy and ask. I realize that sometimes the servants of ladies like Miss Mariah are expected to act as spies for their...protectors. But I assure you that this household was not run that way. Nor would I allow it to be run that way in the future."

John nodded. "I understand. And if this were not an emergency, I would never dare ask you to invade her privacy. Please, I beg of you, speak to the other servants, especially her lady's maid. If you hear anything, I will be going to Miss Manning's directly."

The butler shifted. "Is she truly in danger?"

John nodded as he ran for the door. "I pray not."

But as he swung up on the horse he had abandoned in the drive, he knew in his heart that those prayers were not to be realized. He only hoped he could find her and that she would not be ripped from him.

~

The first thing John noticed as he rode up to Vivien's home was that the guard he had hired to watch her was sitting on his horse across the street. For a moment, his heart soared. If the guard was here, Mariah had to be here, as well. She had to be safe and the necklace that had been sent to him was a cruel hoax.

But there was something deep inside of him that nagged, telling him all was not what it seemed.

He rode up next to the man and pulled to a sharp stop. The guard started as he recognized John.

"Mr. Rycroft?" he asked. "What are you doing here, sir? I did not expect to see you."

John didn't greet the man. Instead, he simply asked, "Is Mariah inside?"

He nodded. "Yes, sir. She arrived a few hours ago and has not left. You can see her carriage parked in the stable around the side if you lean a bit to the right."

John did so and indeed, her carriage was there. It did little to relieve his tension and he gritted his teeth. "Stay here."

The man called a question after him, but John ignored it. He couldn't stop. He wasn't about to waste time.

He rode across the lane and through Vivien's gate. He swung down and the door opened even as he walked up the stairs. Vivien's servant bowed slightly.

"Miss Vivien is not in residence, sir," he explained.

John staggered back. "No."

The servant blinked. "I beg your pardon?"

"Is Mariah here?" he asked, praying but knowing those prayers were not to be answered.

"No," the servant said with confusion. "She and Miss Vivien left for Lord Edmondstone's estate hours ago."

John did not respond. He did not thank him. He did not do anything but bolt for his horse and ride into the night with an increasing sickness in his heart.

~

The servants tried to stop him when John burst through the door at Edmondstone's ten minutes later. In fact, they tried with much more verve than he had been expecting. As he struggled, at least four footmen grabbed for his arms and lunged for his legs.

Under normal circumstances, he might have retreated from physical battle and instead resorted to a logical explanation. But these circumstances were anything but normal, so he pushed at bodies and elbowed his way through the arguing men.

At the sounds of chaos, Edmondstone himself appeared in the foyer, his face pale and his shirt covered with… John gasped.

"Is that blood?" he asked, forgetting about the men he fought long enough that he was tackled to the floor and held there. He didn't care. All he could do was stare.

Edmondstone held his gaze for a long moment, almost as if he were judging his safety. Finally, he waved off his servants.

"Stop," he said softly. "I don't think we need to worry about Mr. Rycroft. He seems as upset as anyone."

The men stopped struggling with John and slowly backed away, though John was not such a fool that he didn't see they stayed right on the edge of the foyer. They were still ready to attack. He staggered to his feet.

"Rycroft?" Edmondstone said with a shake of his head. "What in God's name—"

"Is it *her* blood?" he repeated, his voice cracking.

Edmondstone looked down at himself, at the red splotches on

his shirt and flinched at the sight, which answered John's question. Nausea turned his stomach and he grabbed for the nearest table to steady himself.

"What are you doing here?" the viscount asked.

"I have burst into three different homes tonight, looking for Mariah Desmond," he said, and realized he was begging. "Please, tell me she lives."

Edmondstone blinked and the shock that had lined his face seemed to fade a fraction. "She lives. I don't know how you know that there was an alternative, but come with me."

He pivoted on his heel back into the parlor he had exited and John followed. There were a dozen or so people milling around in the room and he scanned each face for Mariah to no avail. His frustration and fear continued to rise with each passing second.

Everyone was centered around one area in the room and he headed that way. At his approach, the other occupants of the room, both servants and a few men of the upper class, faded back and John caught his breath.

Mariah lay on the settee, half-propped up on a mound of pillows. Vivien was holding one hand, while a doctor finished bandaging the other as he spoke to her in low tones.

She was nodding, but she wasn't listening. No, her eyes, and her attention, were fully fixed on him. Her face was lined with shock, but also relief at his appearance. She was pale and her face was bruised, but she was alive and his heart soared.

He raced to her side and dropped to his knees in front of her, not caring who saw this display of his feelings for her. Vivien released Mariah's hand and the doctor pursed his lips in annoyance and stepped back to speak with the courtesan for moment, leaving Mariah and John as alone as they were going to get in this house, in this public chamber, with her the center of attention in her current state.

"Mariah," he whispered, unable to manage any other words, any other thoughts, any other sounds but her name.

She reached up with her undamaged hand and touched his cheek. "I'm not hurt."

"I beg to differ," he whispered, brushing a finger over her bruised face and motioning to her hand. "What happened?"

Mariah shifted and her face paled even further. But Vivien had no such hesitation. She spun on John, her lips thin, her eyes dark with emotion and said, "She was attacked, in this very house. In a parlor not ten feet from where we all stood talking about such empty things."

Mariah glanced up at her friend. "It wasn't your fault, Vivien. Please stop torturing yourself."

"I left you alone in there. I convinced you to slip away from your guard," Vivien insisted.

John drew back because tears glistened in the experienced mistress's eyes. He had never seen her like this before. And it only served to highlight the seriousness of the situation.

"I too feel the greatest of responsibility," Edmondstone croaked out. "You came here as my guest, Mariah, and somehow a blackguard was able to obtain entry into my home and attack you, rob you, under my very nose. It sickens me."

"Miss Mariah, may I bring you something?" a servant asked with a half curtsey. "Wine?"

"Tea?" Another chimed in.

"And I must tell you how to tend to that wound," the doctor insisted.

John squeezed his eyes shut. These interruptions kept him from doing what he wanted to do. Talk to Mariah. Hold her. Prove to himself that she truly was whole and alive.

He locked gazes with her and without a word, without explanation or asking for leave, he slipped his arms around her and lifted her into his embrace. She did not protest, though he wasn't certain if her acquiescence came from shock or real acceptance. The others in the room, however, did object.

He heard the sounds of dissension as he carried her from the chamber. Vivien's tone was angry, the doctor's filled with disapproval, servants with their dull rumbling and *tsk*ing. But he ignored it all and stalked into the foyer with her.

At the door, there was a touch on his arm and he turned back to see Edmondstone standing there. The older man looked both irritated and intrigued by this unexpected turn.

He folded his arms. "Rycroft, if you insist on sweeping her away in such dramatic fashion, do you at least have a carriage for her comfort?"

John hesitated. He had taken his horse on his desperate search because of the speed and maneuverability a lone rider possessed in the busy city. But Edmondstone was correct that such a position would offer her no comfort, nor even safety.

"Take my carriage," the viscount said with a shake of his head. He motioned for a footman who ran off to fetch the rig. "It was readied earlier in the night so that I could escort Miss Mariah home."

John tensed as those words sank into his mind. Edmondstone was looking at Mariah with a gentle smile. Mariah blushed, but she didn't turn away from the man. And suddenly her reasons for being here became very clear.

He stared at the viscount with new eyes. He was rumored to be nothing but a good man. He'd had a few lovers long ago, but had treated his late wife with respect, generosity and kindness. Something he would probably repeat, on some scale, with a mistress.

The carriage pulled forward and John shook off those troublesome thoughts.

"Thank you," he said softly.

Edmondstone nodded once and then took Mariah's undamaged hand. "I am deeply sorry, my dear."

"As am I," she said softly.

He released her and watched until the rig pulled away toward John's home.

They were silent on the ride. John wasn't certain why. He had so much to say, but here, in this other man's carriage, with Mariah still pale and shaking from whatever she had endured that night, it didn't seem right to bombard her with questions or demands. Instead, he cradled her against his side, her head in the crook of his shoulder, her arms around his waist as if she feared releasing him. As if he was a lifeline. A role he had always insisted he could not, would not, play for any other person.

But in that moment, he felt how perfectly she fit in his arms, how warm and full of life she was. And he hated that it was because of him that she'd been hurt.

The carriage stopped at his home and he lifted her down as his stunned servants rushed out to greet him. He acknowledged no one but Swanson.

"Please ensure that Lord Edmondstone's carriage is returned to him. And send a rider along to bring my horse back from his home," he said as he carried Mariah into the foyer and straight up the stairs to his bedroom.

Once inside, he set her on the bed and moved to the side board where he poured her a strong scotch. He sat down on the settee and stared at her as she sipped the alcohol with a wince at its potency.

She looked so small on his bed. And with her bruised face and bloody clothing, so fragile.

She shifted beneath his focused regard and finally shook her head. "John, when you appeared in Edmondstone's parlor...it was as if I had called you there, like you had been plucked from some dream."

He squeezed his eyes shut. "A nightmare."

"No," she whispered. "A dream. I may have been surrounded by a dozen helpful people, but in truth, all I wanted was you. And then... you were there. Somehow. Some way. Which makes me wonder what other wishes I should make since they are coming true tonight."

He stared at her. "How can you speak in this way when you were attacked?"

She dipped her chin and her bravado faded to nothing and was replaced by all her pain, all her fear. He saw what she had experienced flash across her face and it broke his heart and crushed him to his very core.

"What happened?" he finally asked. It was the question he had to know the answer to, but the one he feared the most. "Please tell me."

She shook her head. "I remember very little. I turned into something which knocked me unconscious."

"What?" he pressed.

She shut her eyes. "I don't know. A fist, a bar of some kind, the butt of a gun. Something with enough power to render me helpless. I only woke again when he…" She halted and the way her throat worked when she swallowed made him ache. "I woke when my attacker cut my hand."

He turned his head as her words slapped him across the face. "He cut you."

She nodded and her gaze drifted to her bandaged hand. "The blade was so sharp and he seemed to take a great deal of pleasure in hurting me. I tried to scream, but he covered my mouth. He ripped my necklace from my throat and that's all I know. My next memory is waking with Vivien standing over me, screaming for help."

"Did you see his face?" John asked as he clenched his fists at his sides.

She shook her head. "He wore some kind of mask to conceal his identity. I only saw his mouth. His smiling mouth."

He scrubbed a hand over his face. Though he doubted his father would do his own dirty work in this instance, the attack had all the telltale signs of Vaughn Rycroft's interference. Sadistic pleasure in the pain of others was something of a calling card of his.

"John, how did you know that I was hurt?" she whispered. "For I know it wasn't my longing for you that brought you to me."

He shook his head. "No. I wish it were, but it wasn't. I knew you had been injured because…" He hesitated, then dug into his pocket and withdrew her necklace. He unwrapped it and held it out to her. "Because of this."

CHAPTER 16

Mariah stared at the necklace John held out toward her. It was one she knew well. Owen had purchased it for her as one of his first gifts. She wore it whenever she attended a party. And tonight it had been snatched from her neck by a blackguard who beat her, cut her…

"J-John," she whispered as she reached out for the jewelry.

His fingers glided against hers as she took it, but he snatched them away and turned his face with an unmistakable expression of guilt. Her heart sank.

"How do you have this? Why?" she asked, flinching at the sight of her own blood still streaked in some of the crevices of the necklace. Her memories of how it had gotten there were blurry, at best, but terrifying.

He rubbed his hands over his face and looked so tired and worn down that she longed to hold him. But she couldn't. Not until she knew what was going on.

"Your attack tonight was a message to me." He jerked his head toward the necklace. "*That* was the delivery of that message and the reason I went looking for you."

"A message," she repeated, uncertain she fully understood as she stared at the jewelry in her hands.

He shook his head. "I'm so, so sorry, Mariah. So sorry I cannot fully express it."

She leaned over to the small table at his bedside and set the necklace there. Then she swigged the entire glass of scotch and placed the empty tumbler next to the jewelry. When she faced John again, she straightened her shoulders and held his gaze evenly.

"John, you guard your history and your emotions religiously, I know that. But I must have a greater explanation than you have presented thus far. I *must*."

John shifted and Mariah could see how utterly uncomfortable her request...no, her *demand*...made him. But she could also see something to his expression she had never seen before.

He was going to acquiesce. He was going to reveal all he had concealed for so long. He was going to give her that glimpse into himself that she had longed for.

She tensed as she allowed him as long as he needed to prepare for that confession. In truth, she needed a moment to draw breath and calm herself.

"I do owe you what you ask for...and so much more," he murmured, his voice distant. "Forgive me if the telling takes me some time. This is not a story I wished to share with anyone. Ever."

She nodded and slid to the end of the bed. As he watched, she shimmied down and moved to sit on the settee beside him. Wordlessly, she took his hand. He stared at their intertwined fingers for a long moment before he cleared his throat.

"You certainly remember when my brother intruded upon us in my home a short time ago," he said.

She nodded. "I do. You did not wish to speak of it."

"No, I did not. We have been estranged for a very long time. The reason is..." he hesitated and his voice barely carried as he said, "The reason is our father. I'm certain you must know that his name is

Vaughn Rycroft. He is the youngest son of the Duke of Lynnmore and was raised in great privilege. He…and the rest of us…were disowned from that family decades ago, but the connection remains and *that* is how my father began his fortune. He increased it via a plethora of cheats and plans, as well as the occasional good investment."

Mariah shifted. A good mistress did investigate her lover's history, but she had not been able to find much more than bare facts in John's. Clearly there was much more to it.

"How did your father cause an estrangement?" she asked softly.

He squeezed his eyes shut. "Many men are disowned from their families, but the reason my father lost his connections was because of his uncommon cruelty. He is like an animal—nothing is too low for him. He destroyed my mother, sending her to live on the street and die alone. I don't even know where she was buried. He spent his life brutalizing his children. His servants. His workers. Anyone he could bully, he exerted his control in the darkest and most painful ways, only to prove he could."

Mariah flinched. Here she had spent years wondering at John's past and the truth of it was as painful as anything she had ever heard. Even without the benefit of fine detail, there was no denying that what he said conjured the most painful and terrible images of two frightened children, ruled by a man on the edge of madness. A man driven to control or destroy.

"John," she whispered and squeezed his hand gently.

He allowed it, but Mariah could see that he barely felt the comfort she hoped to offer in her touch. His expression was too far away, too lost in memories she could not share.

"He was, and is, a bastard of the highest order. Not by birth, but by action. He will hurt. He will steal. He will destroy if it gets him what he desires. He sees himself as king, with everyone else in his life as pawns on his chessboard. He has sacrificed a great many people in order to further his cause. And that included destroying any relationship my brother and I might have had."

Mariah stared at him. She had known John as long as she had

known Owen, but she had never seen him this way. His pain was palpable, and it was made worse by the fact that he hid it always behind that dashing veneer.

"Why did your brother come to you?" she asked. "Especially if you two had been at odds for so long."

He sighed. "My father bestowed his entire fortune on my brother some time ago. It was a way to punish me, and the reason for our initial falling out."

Mariah drew back. "I cannot picture you fighting over something as petty as money."

"It wasn't about money," he said with a shake of his head. "I was already building my fortune when he removed my inheritance. I didn't care about that. But I did care, very much, that he would have my brother under his thumb in such a powerful way. We quarreled. My father convinced Adam that it was my greed that drove my concerns. And Adam, who always longed to see the best in our father, took his side."

Mariah dipped her head. "I can well imagine how painful that must have been."

In truth, she could more than imagine it. Her own family had separated themselves from her once her virtue had no longer been a bargaining chip for them. She had tried so many times to reconcile with them, but they had no interest in associating themselves with a woman they identified as a "whore". Over the years, she had come to terms with that, but there was no joy in it. So she understood loss.

"When he came to me that afternoon, it was because our father had, in turn, cut *him* off. Adam…" He looked at her. "That is my brother's name…*Adam*…he came with a warning that Vaughn Rycroft was turning his eye toward me again. And he was right, for our father visited me not two days ago with all his demands and attempts at control. When I rebuffed him, he turned those threats toward those I cared for. And I believe…no, I *know*, that the attack against you was to prove that he could find a way to reach anyone I lo—"

He broke off with a shake of his head. Mariah stared. His truncated sentence could only end one way, but the sentiment was not directed at her, of course. She had been a pawn to Vaughn Rycroft, a test of what John could expect toward those he truly loved. He certainly didn't count her as one of them. It was not possible.

His shoulders slumped and he shook his head.

"I should have known he would take his threats as far as they would go. I should have protected you."

She cupped his cheeks with her hands. "Look at me."

He blinked and his gaze settled on her for the first time since he began his confession. His dark eyes swirled with pain. Pain she wished to take away, even though she couldn't.

"John, you *tried* to protect me. You put a guard on me." She shook her head. "But I did not understand the gravity of the situation and I found a way to escape him. This was not your fault."

He shoved away from her to his feet. "But it was. I should have told you the moment my father threatened you. Instead, I protected myself by keeping the truth from you. I should have known that you, in all your headstrong glory, would not accept the protection from some unnamed threat."

He shook his head and paced to the fire. "My father has taken everything, all I ever held dear. I refuse to allow him one more moment, one more person, one more fraction of my soul."

She stared at him. His voice was cracking, though she doubted he even recognized it and she could no longer hold back and respect his clear desire for space. She pushed to her feet and moved across the room to him. Wrapping her arms around him, she held to him as tears streamed down her face.

"John," she whispered. "I'm so sorry."

He looked down at her and gently swiped the tears from her cheeks. "Don't."

She shook her head. "How can I not?"

His fingers hesitated against her skin and he stared down at her with an intensity that held her in her place and kept her from breathing or thinking or doing anything except looking at him and seeing everything and everywhere she had ever wanted to be.

Without thinking, she leaned up and gently brushed her lips to his. She felt him hesitate, but then he returned the kiss, holding her so gently that it was as if he thought she would break. He brushed his lips back and forth against hers with a tenderness she had never experienced before.

But as much as she craved that tenderness, she craved something else more. Him.

She parted her lips and demanded more from the kiss as she darted her tongue between his lips and tasted him.

He jerked back as if burned and stared at her. "After tonight—" he began.

She shook her head. "John, tonight I have experienced a great deal of guilt and fear. If I could end this terrible day with pleasure and comfort, I would very much like to feel those things. With you. For both of us. I think we deserve to lose ourselves a little tonight."

He pinched his lips together and she could see that he was thinking of all the reasons why they couldn't, shouldn't, wouldn't, but then he shook his head. He cupped her chin and tilted her face toward his.

"Will you tell me to stop if you don't want this anymore?" he whispered.

"If I didn't want this," she said, just as softly. "I would tell you. But I do want it and you. Always. I ask you to please take me, claim me, make me forget."

His jaw set, working with some kind of struggle against what she asked, but in the end it seemed he was as helpless to their bond as she was. He returned his mouth to hers and kissed her once more. This time, she had no doubt that the kiss would end in so much more.

With a shiver, she wrapped her arms around his neck and leaned into him. The terror of the night melted away as he lifted her against him and carried her to his bed. He kissed her as he laid her across his pillows and took a place beside her.

"Let me help you with your gown," he offered as he began to unbutton the dress. They both looked at the satin fabric, splotched and splattered with blood. "I'll have it destroyed," he said softly, "and another brought here by morning."

She nodded. Certainly, she did not wish to ever see that dress again, even if copious scrubbing *could* make the bloodstains go away. She would always see them there, splashed across the silk.

When she was in a seated position, he slid the gown away from her shoulders and down around her waist, leaving her only in her thin chemise. She lay back down and he removed the rest of the gown to toss it on the floor beside the bed. Then he stared at her.

Mariah had been seen in so many intimate positions in her life. Long ago, she had lost any shame she had in her body or in the pleasures of sex and sin. But here, with John examining her so closely in the firelight, she actually felt…girlish. As if she had never been touched before. Heat burned her cheeks and she fought a strange desire to cover herself.

And yet, perhaps it wasn't strange. She loved John. Acceptance of that fact had finally settled upon her and she no longer tried to deny it, even to herself. So when he looked at her, it was as if she were being seen for the first time. His opinion of her mattered more. She wanted to please him in every way.

"You are the most beautiful woman," he murmured, almost more to himself than to her.

"Even battered and bruised," she teased, if only to lighten the emotion that suddenly hung between them, never to be spoken since it would never be returned.

He frowned. "You are alive. In those moments I thought you weren't…" He shuddered as he reached out to gently drag his fingertips along her cheek. "No, even these marring bruises are beautiful. They mean you survived. And that means more to me than anything in the world at present."

She parted her lips to respond, but the only words she could think of were a declaration of her feelings. So instead, she kissed him. Let him feel her love in her body because she could never say it.

With a groan he glided his fingers into her hair and tilted her head for greater access to her lips. He kissed her and kissed her for what seemed like an eternity and soon she lost track of all time, lost track of everything except for how her body ripened beneath his touch and readied itself for a joining she wanted more than anything.

Except that this didn't feel like their typical sexual encounter, overflowing with passion and desire and wicked intent. There was something gentle about it. Something emotional. But she couldn't dare believe that and put it from her mind as she reached up to unbutton his shirt as best she could with a bandaged hand.

He drew back and looked at her with a frown that was filled with the guilt he continued to insist plague him, and there was a moment's terror that he would pull away entirely. But to her relief, he instead stripped himself of his own shirt, followed by his boots and trousers in short order.

The next time he lay down beside her on the bed, he was more naked than she was and she shivered as his bare skin touched hers.

"Cold?" he asked, moving for a thin blanket draped at the end of the bed.

She caught his hand and lifted it to her breast. "No, not cold," she murmured.

He smiled and the wickedness that had been in check returned in that instant. He cupped her breast lightly, massaging the flesh with just the right amount of pleasing pressure that made her gasp with the feel of it. As her back arched, he began to brush her nipple through her chemise with the back of his hand, teasing the sensitive tip over and over again.

"John," she whispered as she turned her head on the pillow and squeezed her eyes shut at the gathering sensation.

"I've always been amazed at how responsive you remain," he murmured as he lowered his head to her breast.

Through the chemise, he blew a gust of hot air that stimulated her even further. She gripped the bedsheets with both fists and gasped out her approval of his attentions.

In response, he sucked her nipple hard between his lips, swirling his tongue around the fabric of her chemise until it was translucent and she was hardly breathing from pleasure.

"Like that," he chuckled as he withdrew. "I could almost make you come that way. And you're not even naked."

She opened her eyes and smiled at him. "If anyone could, it would be you. All that wicked energy focused on me...I hardly know what to do with it."

"Oh, you know," he growled and placed both hands on her thighs.

He locked gazes with her and slid his hands upward. Her flimsy chemise glided up over her skin, revealing her sex, revealing her belly and finally he let it gather just below the breasts he had been lavishing with his attention a moment before.

"But if I want to make you come," he said, his gaze still locked with hers, "I know a way."

She opened her legs. He hadn't asked her to, but she had to. She needed him so badly that her body was weeping, her knees were shaking, and the only way to obtain her desire was to give herself over to him. Tonight, she would let him pleasure her. She would let her own needs trump anything else, because he allowed her, nay expected her, to do so.

And who was she to deny him?

He finally broke their gaze and looked down at her sex, presented to him now slick and hot. He shuddered before he pressed a finger against her clitoris and rubbed a circle around the delicate, sensitive nub of nerves.

Mariah cried out as a shocking burst of pleasure cascaded from the place he touched her through her sex, through her limbs, to everyplace that was sensitive and raw on her body.

"Yes, *that* is how I'll make you come," John said, his voice rough. "But not yet. Not yet."

He removed his finger and her body ached in response, lifting toward him of its own accord and causing her to whimper most plaintively.

"When?" she whispered.

He chuckled and lowered himself between those same legs. As he spread her sex open, he breathed a hot stream of air against her wet sex.

"Soon," he promised and then stroked his tongue over her entrance.

Although he pointedly avoided her clitoris, that did not mean that he did not pleasure her. With every lick, he seemed to light her on fire. With each stroke he had her rolling her hips to find more pleasure, to demand more of his tongue and his fingers and his body.

She had been pleasured so many times before, but tonight it felt different. Perhaps because of the fear from earlier in the evening. Perhaps because she was too exhausted and injured to try to offer as much pleasure as she gave.

Or perhaps because this was a man she loved and he was giving her something to comfort her. To please her. Something that required no reciprocity.

"John," she whispered, her voice broken by emotion and pleasure.

He lifted his gaze and met her eyes from between her legs. His sensual, self-satisfied expression made her shiver at the edge of orgasm.

"I want you...inside of me," she whispered. "Now."

"No more of this?" he questioned, his tongue darting out and finally stroking her clitoris.

She let out a strangled moan, but shook her head. "You. Just you."

His expression softened, but he obliged, rising up over her to cover her with his warmth and protection. She put her arms around him and closed her eyes as he glided deep within her in one slick stroke. She came almost instantly, and with a power that took her off guard. She had no control over the lift of her hips, the squeeze of her pussy against his cock. Her cries echoed in the air and the nails of her uninjured hand dug into his shoulder as she rode out the quick, hot, powerful orgasm he had created and now dragged out with each long, satisfying stroke.

And he seemed no more immune to her than she was to him. As her orgasm faded, his strokes increased, becoming erratic, becoming wild until he grunted her name and poured his seed deep into her body.

~

John smiled as Mariah settled back against the pillows, her face glowing from release and pleasure. At least he could give her that. A small trade off considering all she'd lost thanks to him. Thanks to his father.

He slid away from the bed and retrieved his robe. As he tied it, she sat up, lifting the sheets to cover her bare breasts.

"You are leaving?" she asked, a lilt of panic to her tone.

He turned at her desperate voice and shook his head. "No. No, I'm only going to make the arrangements for your gown." She relaxed a bit, but he could see she was still on edge. Fearful.

She needed him. And he was damn well going to be here this time.

"Rest," he said softly. "I'll join you in just a moment. And tomorrow...*tomorrow* we will talk more about what to do now that you know the truth about how deep a threat my father is to you."

She hesitated a moment, but then nodded. He turned to go to the door, but her voice stopped him.

"John?" she said. When he looked at her, she smiled. "I don't blame you."

He nodded and continued toward the door. As he rang for the servant, he heard her yawn behind him, and by the time he looked at her, she had rested her head onto the pillows and was already drifting off to sleep.

She might not blame him *yet*. But after tomorrow, she might very well feel differently. Especially if the plan he was now formulating to keep her safe was the only one his mind could conceive.

CHAPTER 17

John looked up as the door to the breakfast room opened and Mariah slipped inside, wearing the gown that had been delivered in the middle of the night.

He caught his breath at the sight of her, despite his attempts not to react. The bruising to her face had grown worse since last night and her hand was swollen beneath the bandages as she held it against her stomach.

She had been smiling upon her entry, but his reaction made her expression fall.

"We did the best we could to cover the worst of it," she whispered as her cheeks darkened with embarrassment. "I know I look a fright."

He pushed to his feet and moved to the doorway where she lingered. He gently cupped her chin and lifted it so she would look into his eyes.

"I am glad you are alive," he said. "The bruises will fade, your hand will heal…"

He trailed off because he realized she would probably have an ugly scar on that hand to remind her of last night forever. One more item to add to his list of fault in this situation.

"Now come," he said with false brightness as he motioned to the table. "Eat. You need your strength."

She took the hand he offered and the seat he pulled out for her. Once she was settled, he returned to his place beside her and glanced at her. She was staring at her plate, her expression blank and faraway. Blank except for the pain there.

He shifted. He was responsible for all of this. Every time he looked at her, that fact became clearer. And since her situation was his fault, he was the only one who could resolve it.

The servants set a plate of food before her, but she made no move to touch it. He waited until they were alone before he spoke again.

"Mariah, I have thought of what happened to you all night."

She flinched, but then a false smile tilted her lips. "Not all night, I don't think. You were rather more pleasantly occupied for a good portion of the evening."

He sucked in a breath. Mariah had never put on her "mistress" face with him. The one that deterred all true connection, that played off her own feelings or needs in order to bow to the needs of her protector. But he saw her doing it now. And it killed him to know she was trying so hard to make this right for him.

"Mariah, please," he said, placing a hand over hers. "I need to talk to you about this seriously and honestly."

She jerked her gaze to his in surprise, but then she nodded. "Y-Yes. Of course."

He cleared his throat, but did not remove his hand from hers. "I did not sleep last night as I went over every way I could think of to protect you. But my father wants to hurt me by hurting you. There is no getting around that. I cannot allow him to do that again, for I fear his attempts against you will only become more violent."

She snatched her hand away and stared at him. "You think he would pursue me again?"

He nodded. "Yesterday I played into his hand. I panicked. My fear, my desperation, they would have been obvious to anyone who encountered me, including the spies who were no doubt following me as I raced from one home to another, seeking you out. Their reports would have given the old man great pleasure, and more ammunition."

She shook her head. "But now that we know…"

He raised a hand. "Yes, of course, the knowledge that he is willing to go so far gives us a greater ability to defend ourselves, to defend *you*. But I fear it won't be enough."

She stared at him. "You think he would go further than he did last night?"

"I know he would," John whispered.

"Then you are saying you must end this between us," she said, turning her face and staring at her rapidly cooling food. "To take away any ammunition our relationship may give him."

John shifted. "I—I had thought of that, yes. Of course, separating from you would seem to be the best route, but I don't think that would stop him. He knows that I…that *we* have a deeper connection. Even if we aren't together, hurting you will hurt me. If we end our affair, all I fear it will succeed in doing is putting you more at risk. Especially once he realizes I *will* bend to him when you are threatened."

She lifted her gaze and John was shocked to see joy in her expression. "So you aren't walking away?"

He drew back. In the midst of the most dangerous position she had probably ever been in, Mariah was only thinking of their relationship. That she could take any pleasure in it anymore was a testament to her, and a source of even more guilt for him.

"No," he said. "I could not now."

"Then what do you suggest?" she asked.

"I have destroyed your life," he said. "Your chances at finding another protector have been materially damaged by me and my family. There is but one solution."

She blinked. "And that is?"

For a flash of a moment, John realized he should get down on one knee for this. That he should be romantic or emotional. He did not do any of those things.

"You shall marry me."

~

There was only one explanation Mariah could come to as she stared at John. She had to have been hit harder on the head than she thought and now she was involved in some kind of strange waking dream. One where she got something she had secretly wanted but never admitted to herself until John said those words.

Except she *couldn't* have that. If this was a dream, it certainly wasn't the most romantic proposal ever. In truth, he looked quite sick about it. So what was real and what was fantasy?

"M-Marry," she managed to force herself to say as she shifted in her seat, which was suddenly very uncomfortable. "You cannot mean that. Mistresses do not marry."

John shook his head sadly. "I'm afraid this state of affairs has gone far beyond mistresses and the empty label of 'protector' that men of my status wear when they take on a lover. You need someone to *truly* protect you."

She swallowed, her tongue thick and dry in her mouth. "And you believe somehow that a marriage between us will allow you to do that."

He hesitated and that pause spoke volumes about how distasteful he found this suggestion. Still, eventually he nodded.

She pushed to her feet and wobbled slightly. Exhaustion, the events of last night and this final shocking interaction with John had all taken their toll. She balanced herself against the table edge before she paced to the fireplace and stared into the flames. Anything not to look at him and see how little he wanted her.

"How?" she whispered.

"I would be able to protect you financially and physically. In my home, I can provide far better security."

She shifted. "Then why not simply officially take on a role as my protector rather than marry me?" she asked. "Certainly you could provide financial and physical protection to me as a mistress."

He shook his head. "It will not be enough. You'll still be seen as vulnerable. As my wife, you will have my legal protection. It is one thing for my father to attack a…a…"

She blinked. "Whore?"

He flinched. "I do not think of you that way and I never have."

She shrugged. "But the law sees me as little better."

He hesitated, but there was nothing he could do but nod. "However, once we are married you take on the role of a gentleman's wife. Even a man with as much power as my father cannot turn violence on you without recourse."

She opened her mouth, but there was no arguing with such a point. It was utterly and completely true. Once married, she would be seen very differently than she was now. At least by the law.

"Mariah," he continued as he took a step toward her, though he made no effort to touch her. "If we do this, you need never worry about your future in any way ever again. And I will resolve this issue with my father, I promise you."

She pursed her lips as she examined him carefully. He was so utterly, ridiculously handsome and he stared at her with so much wanting in his eyes. *Wanting* to protect her. *Wanting* to right whatever wrong he felt he'd done by having this man as his sire.

She did not see, however, that he wanted to keep her because he cared for her. So while she should have been happy that the man she loved was offering to make her his bride, she was most decidedly *not*.

Her body felt very weak suddenly and she eased herself to the chair she had vacated. When her vision stopped swimming, she said, "Let us suppose you are somehow able to stop your father and in a week or a month or a year, we deem that I am safe. What then?"

He blinked and there was true confusion on his face. "I'm afraid I don't understand."

She shut her eyes. Of course he didn't. It wasn't as if he had thought this through beyond keeping her from being physically injured.

"What happens once this is resolved?" she pushed. "We will be married. And?"

He shook his head. "Well, you will be my wife."

She sighed. "Will I be, John? Will I be your wife in any real way?"

She could see the answer in the way he flinched, the way he shifted, the way he swallowed hard before he answered.

"In every way I could allow you to be."

The sentence repeated in her head. *In every way I could allow you to be.*

It was no answer.

"I don't know," she said, covering her eyes with her hands. "I must think. I cannot think."

He moved toward the table, his eyes flashing with emotions much deeper than any he had ever shown toward her in the past.

"No, there is no time to think, Mariah. Last night should have shown you that."

She threw up her hands. "Dear God, John! Are you truly so cold that you cannot see how transformative this decision will be for me?"

"Mariah," he sighed, his tone filled with irritation, but she did not allow him another word.

"Perhaps your existence would not significantly change if you took a wife, any wife, even *me* as your wife," she continued. "But mine will change in every way. You are asking me to leave the life I know and in trade you'll offer me some kind of protection against harm, but little else. This is not something I can consider lightly."

"How could you miss the life you know?" he asked in stunned disbelief. "A life where you must depend upon a man's discretion for your funds, your home, your very existence."

She arched a brow. "And that would change, how?"

His lips thinned. "I don't know if other men treat their wives like mistresses, but I would not. You would have guarantees. You would never need worry about…well, anything ever again."

"What about children?" she whispered.

That drew him up short. "I—I had not considered that."

"No, I thought not." She shook her head. "What about Society?"

He blinked. "What about it?"

She gritted her teeth. "I assume as your wife that I would take on some duties in your home. Would your associates and friends accept a woman who once turned up her skirts in trade for protection? Would their wives?"

He hesitated again. "I don't know."

She threw up her hands. "You see, there is more for me to consider than you, I suppose. Please give me at least twenty-four hours to do so."

She folded her arms and stared up at him, determined not to be seduced or bullied into such an altering decision. Especially when her head was swimming and she still wasn't entirely certain if this was reality or a dream.

"Mariah," he growled, low and still highly emotional.

But whatever he was going to say was lost as there was a light knock on the door and then Swanson entered.

"I'm sorry to intrude, sir, but Miss Vivien Manning is here and she demands to see Miss Mariah."

Mariah squeezed her eyes shut. Thank God for Vivien and her impeccable timing.

Obviously John thought something much different. She was sure she heard him utter a curse beneath his breath before he waved at his servant.

"Fine. Let her in."

Swanson backed from the room and in a moment, he returned with Vivien at his side. She gave him no time to announce her, but burst into the dining room and straight to Mariah's side for a tight, hard hug that all but sucked the air from her lungs.

"Thank God," Vivien whispered against her hair.

"I'm all right," Mariah responded as her friend released her and instead turned her attention, in the form of a dark glare, on John.

"How could you sweep her away like that?" Vivien demanded, her face dark pink. "How *dare* you? Did you even ensure that the wrappings on her wound were properly changed?"

John straightened his shoulders and Mariah could see he remained angry and frustrated, and probably as much at her as at her friend.

"Of course I did. What do you take me for?"

Vivien folded her arms. "I do not rightly know anymore, John Rycroft."

He stood staring at the two women for a long moment, but then he stalked across the room to the door.

"I'll leave you to each other since it's evident I am not needed here. But, Vivien, talk some sense into your friend." He locked eyes with Mariah. "Perhaps you are the only one who can."

With that, he slammed the door behind himself and left Mariah alone with Vivien.

CHAPTER 18

Vivien collapsed into the seat beside Mariah and stared at her friend. Mariah drew back in surprise. The other woman's eyes were rimmed with black circles and bright red from what could be nothing else but tears.

"Dear God," she said as she took Vivien's hand with her uninjured one. "You did not stay up all night fretting over me, did you?"

Vivien stared at her in disbelief.

"How could I not? You were brutally attacked in a room just down the hall from me, I *found* you in a pool of your own blood and then John swooped in and carried you away, leaving everyone to wonder what in the world was going on. Selfish man!"

Mariah squeezed her friend's hand gently. Although she currently had much the same sentiment about John, she could not help but defend him nonetheless.

"Don't be too hard on John," she said softly. "He has his reasons for what he did."

Vivien scoffed and released Mariah's hand to pace to the window. She looked out over the street for a few minutes before she turned with a shake of her head. "And what did he mean with his parting words? What sense must I talk you into?"

Mariah shifted. As much as she wanted to tell her friend every-thing, the situation was complicated. Vivien would most certainly scold her.

"What is going on?" she asked with wide eyes when too much silence stretched between them.

Mariah shrugged. "It is nothing of consequence."

"Bollocks!" her friend burst out in a rare flash of temper. "You owe me honesty after last night, so tell me this instant."

"I do." Mariah folded her arms. "I'm sorry. John has...he has proposed marriage to me."

Vivien stood stock-still for a long moment, then moved to the closest chair and sank down in it with a thud. She stared at Mariah the entire time, her gaze boring into her like a tool through wood.

"I am going to get a reputation," her friend finally muttered.

Mariah smiled at that quip. One of Vivien's other matches between mistress and protector had just resulted in a marriage. But those were far different circumstances. A love match.

Her smile fell. "His reasons for asking me are not due to some romantic notion, I assure you."

Vivien tilted her head. "No?"

Mariah lifted her eyebrows at her friend's expression. "Why do you look and sound so surprised by the facts? You know our situation."

Vivien laughed, though there was little humor to the sound. "No, my dear. I do not. In truth, I think you two have as little notion about it as anyone. But if John has not admitted an attachment, then why would he ask you to be his bride?"

Mariah sighed. If she had come so far, there was no need to hide the truth any longer.

"The attack on me last night," she said softly. "It was...because of him. Or so he thinks. Because of his family. And he has convinced himself that marriage is the only way he can protect me until he can deal with his..."

She broke off. This was John's secret and his pain, not hers to tell, even to her best friend.

"His father?" Vivien asked when she did not finish her sentence. "Is it Vaughn Rycroft who hurt you?"

Mariah's eyes widened. "How do you know that?"

She shivered. "A woman in my position would be foolish not to know the dangerous men as well as the rich. I've heard tales of him, vague but disturbing. And *he* arranged your attack?"

Mariah shrugged. "So John believes."

Vivien returned her gaze to the window. It had begun to rain and droplets clung to the glass like teardrops. She was silent for so long that Mariah stood, believing the exchange to be over.

But her friend surprised her by pivoting around, her face pale, and said, "You should accept his offer."

Mariah gripped at the edge of the table in disbelief. "His offer of marriage?" When Vivien nodded, Mariah continued, "What in the world are you talking about? I would never have thought I would hear those words coming from you!"

"And if this were a normal circumstance, when a gentleman is infatuated with his mistress and offers her a marriage, I would tell her to refuse. Those scenarios rarely work out, and the woman almost always comes to suffer far more. But this offer he makes you is not about love or passion. You could be killed. And I have lost too much, too many people. You are..." Vivien choked and tears sparkled in her eyes. "You are my best friend."

Mariah sucked in her breath in shock as she scurried around the table and embraced Vivien as hard as her friend had embraced her earlier. For a moment, they stood together, silent, their foreheads pressed close.

Then Mariah drew back and Vivien swiped her tears in frustration. "Does that mean you will accept?"

Mariah shivered. "I don't know. It would be one thing to marry someone I did not love, someone who did not love me. We would be on equal ground. But to enter into a union such as this when I feel so much and he so little…"

Vivien wrapped an arm around her. "Think of it this way. If he had asked you to be his mistress today, be your protector rather than marry you, would you have agreed?"

Mariah considered the question. Certainly that was all she had hoped for. And despite her feelings for him, she knew the answer.

"Yes," she admitted. "I would have said yes."

"Then say yes to this," Vivien insisted. "The difference between wife and mistress is not so great as you think."

Mariah pursed her lips. "You must be desperate to try to make me believe such lies," she said. When Vivien shook her head, she lifted a hand to keep her friend from arguing. "Please! I may not be as experienced as you are, but I know what you say isn't true. And so do you."

Vivien's shoulders slumped. "Perhaps you are right. But I urge you to think about accepting nevertheless. With the situation so dire, I beg of you not to dismiss it out of hand."

Mariah nodded and was rewarded by Vivien's relieved smile. But even as she returned the expression, there was a pit in her stomach. If she said yes to such a shocking proposal, the entire situation would end in only one thing— heartache. Hers. And soon.

John was expecting Vivien to burst into his office in a fury, so when she did just that an hour after her arrival to his home, he did not even look up from his paperwork.

"Sit down, Vivien," he said. "Allow me to sign this and you'll have my full attention."

She huffed out her breath, but did as he asked and flopped herself into a chair across from him. She waited, rather patiently, actually, as he signed his name to the missive he'd been writing and handed it off to the same servant who had trailed her into the room.

But once the door was shut behind the man, she did not even allow him a breath before she started in on her inevitable tirade.

"What are you thinking?"

John shut his eyes and pondered all the ways he might remain in control for the next few moments.

"I am not certain to what you refer," he managed through clenched teeth. "Are you angry at me about last night? About the threats against Mariah? Or about the proposal of marriage? I ask because I'm certain you now know about all those things."

Vivien nodded. "I do and I'm angry about all of them, honestly."

"Then this promises to be a most tedious conversation, I shall get myself some brandy." He rose and moved to the sideboard. "Would you like one?"

Her lips pursed, but as he examined her more closely, he could see that anger wasn't her main emotion after all. Concern was what lined her face. Somehow he preferred anger.

"Yes," she snapped, but some of the heat was gone from her voice.

He half-smiled as he poured them each a drink. She sipped hers and motioned for him to return to his chair.

"You are correct that I do know a great deal about the situation now that I've spoken to Mariah." She arched a brow, spoiling for a fight. "Do you judge her so harshly for her need to talk to a friend?"

John hesitated. Normally he would not like the idea of his privacy being invaded, but the circumstances were anything but normal.

"Mariah is under a great deal of strain thanks to…I assume she told you about my father."

"I guessed," Vivien said softly. "I had heard stirrings about his cruelty. Faint, but enough of them to give them a great deal of merit." She set her drink down on the desk and leaned closer. "I hope you know my frustration or worry about this situation has nothing to do with blame. At least not for anything your family has done or may do. You are not at fault for their actions."

She said the same words that Mariah had, but as before, they gave him little comfort.

"I am not the one who needs your assurance," he said, grim. "The fact is that whether or not I am at fault for the man behind these threats, I am responsible for protecting Mariah now that they have occurred. And the best, and perhaps only, way I can do that is to marry her."

Vivien shifted. "You are probably right on that score."

He drew back. "That is certainly a most unexpected reaction. Truly?"

She nodded. "Yes, but, John, I hope you also realize that in the long run there will be more to protect here than just her life once this threat has past. Once she is your wife, there will be...there are other..."

Vivien broke off and grabbed for her drink. She took a long swig and John could see her struggling with whatever message she was trying to send.

"I've never known you to mince around any subject," he said. "Don't start now. What is your concern?"

She folded her arms. "Mariah may have been a mistress to your friend, she may be an experienced lover with you, but there are still parts of her that are very sheltered, innocent. She puts her...her heart into what she does, John. And once she loves, she will love until she breaks."

John nearly dropped his glass as he stared at Vivien. Love?

"Are you telling me that Mariah loves me?"

Those words rolled from his tongue and tasted strangely sweet. But he did not want that. Not from anyone, especially not from her. Not when he could give nothing of the kind back.

Vivien shook her head and she had managed to hood her expression so that he could no longer read her concerns. She got to her feet.

"I am saying nothing except that once she is your wife, your responsibility toward her will no longer only be physical or financial or even sexual. You will make promises to her that go beyond those things. I hope you will try to keep them."

He pushed to his feet. He could not continue this line of discussion with Vivien. He could not even *think* about this line of discussion, truth be told.

"I understand," he choked out with effort. "And I do hope you know me well enough to know I would never hurt Mariah. Not if I could avoid doing so."

Vivien moved to the door, where she paused and turned toward him. "I do know you would try. But I just don't want to see her being kept as a mistress with a ring on her finger. That kind of union will only bring her great pain. Consider it, John, before you act any further."

Then she turned and walked away, not waiting for him or for his servant to show her out. A polite host would have followed her and bid her farewell. But in that moment, John did not feel polite.

He felt confused. Tense.

Vivien had said love, even if she tried to play it off a moment later. If she had said it, she must fear Mariah already felt such a charged and dangerous emotion, or *could* feel it toward him in the future.

No one loved him. He made sure of it. Love was an inconvenient, irrational inclination that had led to more heartache than pleasure. Oh certainly, there were a few people in his acquaintance who seemed very well matched, but they were what, one or two out of a hundred? Those odds were not very good and he had learned how to gamble long ago.

Of course, he did care for Mariah. She was a friend, a lover, he had come to depend upon her and look to her for companionship, as well as passion. But that wasn't love. Was it? Even if it felt like it. Even if the word sometimes bubbled up on his mind unbidden.

He couldn't surrender to it, though. He wasn't capable of all the expectations around it.

And if Mariah *did* have those kinds of feelings for him…the heartache that would likely follow was something he could not protect her from.

Mariah hesitated outside of John's office, standing with her hand lifted but utterly unable to do what she had come to do and knock. Once she did, her entire life, her definition of herself, her very future, would be altered irrevocably.

But what other choice did she have? Everyone important in her life had made it very clear that this was now her only option.

She thrust her hand forward and rapped her knuckles against the smooth surface of the door.

There was a beat of hesitation and then John's distracted voice said, "Come."

She shivered as she entered. He had given her that same order numerous times before, with a very different meaning.

But as she looked at him, sitting at his desk, his gaze focused on a pile of paperwork before him, he did not look much like the passionate lover who dragged her headlong into passion so powerful that it swept her away.

He looked like a lord of the manor. A very important man. And for the first time she got a full glimpse of the entirety of what it would be like to be married to him.

He glanced up at her and the blood drained from his face.

"Mariah?" he said, his voice rough as he staggered to his feet. "I'm sorry, I would have come to you. You should have sent word through Swanson or another servant."

She blinked, forcing herself to focus. "I am not so delicate or damaged that I could not make my way to your office myself, John."

He waved to a seat and then to the sideboard. "May I get you something? Or call for tea?"

She frowned. What was this distance, this formality between them? He could scarcely look at her as he bustled about, trying to tend to her comfort when all she wanted him to do was sit down and talk to her.

"I'm fine," she said firmly and the finality of her tone stopped him.

"Are you?" he asked, his eyebrow arching.

She smiled slightly. There was her John. He was still in there after all.

"Yes," she said softly. "But you are making me dizzy running all around the room like this. Won't you sit?"

She motioned to the chair next to her and hoped he would take it rather than the one with a desk separating them like an impenetrable fortress.

He stared at the chair, then his chair. Then he took the one next to her, though he looked anything but comfortable as he perched there.

"I have a decision for you," she said softly.

He jolted straight in the chair like she had prodded him with some kind of electricity. "What happened to twenty-four hours?"

She pursed her lips. "I needed some space, what with you railing at me and the room spinning sideways. It turns out that once I had it, I did not need twenty-four hours to find my answer. Just a few."

He swallowed. "Then what is your response to my question?"

"I do not wish to saddle you with a bride you clearly do not want," she said softly and refused to look at him so she would not see the agreement to that statement. "But you are right that I have not the resources to protect myself from the kind of threats that now rain down on me."

When she dared to look, she saw his frown had deepened, but he did not interrupt her.

"You say you can," she hurried to continue. "And if this is your only option for doing that, I would be a fool to refuse. I *will* marry you, John, if you still believe this course is for the best."

He was so quiet for so long that Mariah had no choice but to finally look at him. He was staring, not at her face but at her bandaged hand. Just staring at it, as if he could will it well by gazing at it with such intensity.

"John?" she whispered. "Is this still your suggested route or am I making an utter cake of myself by bringing up the subject?"

He jerked his gaze to hers and nodded. "Yes." When she tilted her head in confusion, he clarified. "Yes, to this being the best course. No, you are not making a cake of yourself."

She relaxed, at least a little. "Good. I would have felt very foolish if you had changed your mind."

He reached out and traced her jaw with his fingertips. "No. There is no going back now."

He leaned closer and she let her eyes flutter shut. At least he would kiss her. He would be hers to kiss her whole life. There was something very pleasant about that fact.

But instead of kissing her mouth, he brushed his lips against her cheek and then drew back. When he smiled, there was nothing true about it. He was a distant man being polite to a fiancée who had been arranged for him by forces out of his control.

And her breakfast stirred in her stomach quite unpleasantly.

"I shall begin making the arrangements right away," he said as he got to his feet and moved away from her. Just around the desk, but it might as well have been all the way around the world. "And you should rest. The next few weeks will be eventful indeed."

"Indeed," she repeated, but her tone was flat and pained to her own ears. Somehow, though, she managed to get up and back from the room. Before she was even gone, he had returned to his books.

And she realized in that moment that she had lost him.

CHAPTER 19

Mariah flexed her hand. After a few days, she no longer had to have her cut bandaged, a freedom she welcomed. She stared at the line that remained red across her palm. It certainly represented a great deal of pain. Not physical pain, or at least not much more now than a twinge now and then, an itch as the skin reformed itself into what she assumed would be a fairly substantial scar.

No, when she looked at the mark, it was a reminder of the terror of that night and a signal of the beginning of her marriage as much as the ring John would put on her finger in…she shut her eyes…just under a week now. He had been pulling strings and making inquiries to rush that process for days.

So much so that they had barely seen each other, barely talked, barely interacted at all since she accepted his proposal.

In the past, she'd sometimes heard the few married ladies who sneaked into Vivien's manor complain about the way a husband treated a wife. The neglect. The utter lack of care beyond producing an heir. Mariah had always taken a little comfort in the fact that the particular end those women described would never be hers. If a man tired of his mistress, he settled her well and they both walked away. She with her independence furthered, he with his conscience clear.

That couldn't happen once a wedding took place. Oh, she and John might be able to lead separate lives, but she would never again be truly independent because she would share his name and his purse. An allowance would be awarded to her, a generous one she was certain, but that was not the same as an account no one but she could access. A home that was separate. A life she called her own.

Mariah shook her head and got to her feet to pace around the room to the window. Outside, the city lights glittered and reminded her that at this time of night a week ago she would have been in John's bed, making love to him with abandon.

Not anymore.

But her wayward thoughts judged John more harshly than she meant to do. After all, she had faith in him that he would never be anything but kind to her. Even during the past few days, when he had installed her into a bedroom separate from his own and avoided any meaningful contact with her, he had been *kind*.

But she hated to think that after the passion they had shared, "kindness" was all she could expect for the next twenty or thirty or fifty years of her life. That somehow her role as wife would wipe away any remnants of the other roles she had once filled for him—lover…friend…

She squeezed her eyes shut and pictured John coming toward her, John pressing his mouth to hers. John's body pressed against her. Inside of her.

A shiver racked her as she jerked her eyes open.

"If you want it, take it," she whispered.

That was a mantra Vivien often repeated to her. One she did not often dare to live up to. Except now, those words seemed her only option. If she wanted John, and if she wanted to remind him that he wanted her too, she would have to be the one who seduced. Who claimed.

Otherwise, she would be facing a very sad union, indeed.

She pushed away from the window and stepped into the hallway. There she found Swanson, speaking to one of the extra men John had hired to guard his home. She blushed as the large, burly guard looked over Swanson's shoulder at her. Sizing up the merchandise, no doubt, to see if it was worthy of his protection. His blank expression revealed nothing of his answer on that score.

Swanson spun around at the guard's distraction and smiled at her.

"Ah, Miss Mariah." He did not look at the guard again, but said over his shoulder, "You may take your place outside. Please recall your instructions."

The man grunted and moved away from the hall and into the foyer where Mariah heard the front door close behind him.

"Has having more men working for the household made your job more difficult?" she asked.

The butler tilted his head in surprise. "No. No, Miss Mariah, of course not. They are rough men and must be handled somewhat differently than I would handle a footman or maid, but there is no extra work for me. Even if there were, I believe your safety would be worth that burden."

Mariah smiled. Society at large might never accept her, John might begin to look upon her as a burden he regretted taking, but clearly Swanson and the rest of the servants were determined to make her a welcome lady of the household. A small step, but one that gave her a little confidence, at least, that the future was conquerable.

"And has Mr. Rycroft already gone to bed, or is he in his office?" she asked.

Swanson shifted slightly. "I believe Mr. Rycroft is finishing up some work in his office, but he has told me he plans to go to his chamber within the half hour."

"I see," Mariah shifted. "Is his valet to be sent up to him soon?"

"In ten minutes, yes, to await his arrival."

Mariah met the other man's eyes. "Perhaps that order could be ignored?" she said softly. "Or perhaps you could just assume that *someone* will be present to play the role of valet for Mr. Rycroft?"

Swanson hesitated and she could see that the concept of ignoring a direct request from his master was a foreign one. But then he nodded. "It seems to me that as long as Mr. Rycroft has what he needs, there is no reason for anyone in the household to interfere. Do *you* require anything of me, miss?"

Confidence sprang to mind, but she doubted the butler kept an extra cup of that in his shirtwaist, so she merely shook her head.

"No. I think I will head upstairs now. I have no need for my maid."

"Good night, miss." The butler gave a low bow.

Mariah smiled at the man and then headed upstairs to wait for John. And prayed that her wiles would be irresistible to him. If they were not, she didn't know how she could face a lifetime of his disregard after a few weeks of his utter devotion and desire.

John was still reading a missive that had come to him late in the evening when he entered his bedchamber at midnight. He turned the page and continued to read even as he nudged the door shut behind him.

"Mr. Thomason?" he called out as he shook his head. "I believe I must make a call tomorrow. Will you be certain my green waistcoat is repaired? That button was loose last time I wore it."

When there was no reply from his normally competent valet, he set the letter aside on the nearest table and looked around the room. There was something not quite right. His fire was too low, his dressing room too quiet. Had Swanson not sent up the valet? How could that be? Swanson was always the picture of perfect service.

He turned toward the bell to ring for his valet himself when a soft sound from his bedroom stopped him.

"Perhaps you could simply wear a different waistcoat."

John stared at the bell next to his door for a long, charged moment. He wanted to turn around so badly he could taste the anticipation sweet on his tongue. It tasted like the soft skin of the woman who had just spoken to him. A woman who should very much not be in his bedroom. Not because she wasn't wanted there, but because she was wanted far too much.

"What are you doing, Mariah?" he asked as he finally allowed himself to turn toward her.

Any further questions died on his lips, for when he faced her, he found that she was utterly naked. Except for his dressing gown, which was opened in the front to reveal all the pale, firm flesh of her body that could inspire a damned novel.

One that would *not* be read by ladies of good breeding.

"I am visiting my lover in his chamber," she explained as she leaned back against the doorway separating the two chambers of his room. She arched her back and the robe gaped a fraction to reveal the curve of her breast, complete with a hard, pink nipple at the tip. One he wanted to latch on to with his lips and suckle until she slid to the floor in a heap.

"I'm not your lover," he reminded her. And himself. Mostly himself. "I'm your fiancé now."

"Yes," she said and then pondered him closely. "And it seems you do not believe they could possibly be one and the same. Despite everything."

"Because of everything," he insisted and moved toward her without wanting to do so.

She tilted her head. "I don't understand."

He rubbed his eyes with one hand, but the image of her naked body never left his mind even if he wished to scrub it free.

"You are to be my wife," he tried to explain. "And if anyone is ever going to respect you, I must be the one to set that precedent. And the first step is to treat you as I would treat a fiancée from my own class. I would not...I would not..."

He opened his eyes and stared at her. If he said out loud all the things he would not do, he would find himself doing them. And that was wrong.

Somehow.

He was having a hard time remembering just why when she smiled at him in such a wry, knowing way and turned to face him head-on. Her body was on display and his cock refused to listen to reason, instead hardening until he could scarcely breathe.

"So you would respect me by keeping your hands off of me?" she asked.

He nodded. His mouth was too dry to give another answer. Especially when she slipped her thumbs under the lapel of his robe and shoved it away from her body.

"That is a very sad beginning to a marriage," she whispered. "To show a woman respect by showing her no desire. How much worse will it get when we are married?" She lowered her hand between her legs and stroked there without breaking his gaze. "Will you lock my pussy away in a chastity belt? Will you pass me in the hallway pressed against the wall so you do not touch me?"

He cleared his throat. "You're being ridiculous."

"I'm not." She shimmied closer and the way her hips twitched mesmerized him. "I'm being very realistic. You see, my dear, this marriage you have proposed may not be for fortune or for..." She hesitated for just a fraction. "Or for love. But as your wife, I intend to demand that your husbandly duties be fulfilled in the bedroom. And I am starting now."

She reached him and shoved his jacket off his shoulders with a saucy wink that made his already hard cock even harder.

"Don't make me ask twice," she said as she leaned up to press a heated kiss against his neck.

She was presenting far too tempting a prospect, something John guessed she knew full well. He should have been able to control his reaction to her. After all, beautiful women had thrown their charms at him dozens of times before only to be rebuffed.

The difference was he wanted this woman. Passionately. Powerfully. And he could not deny that when she wound one naked leg around his and arched up against his hard cock with a shiver of desire.

He found his hands lifting, almost of their own accord, winding around her upper arms and dragging her against him fully.

"Oh yes," she purred, rubbing against him like a cat who had discovered a saucer of cream. "This is what I need. I'm pleased you do not intend to deny it to me."

"Deny you?" he growled as he shoved her toward the bed. "Who could dare do that?"

Then there were no more words. He opened her naked legs and gazed down at the glistening sex waiting for him. She was right, he had been avoiding her, but it was only because she was such a temptation. Every moment of every day, he longed to pound deeply into her body. To take her, to claim her, to make her his in more primal a way than any slip of paper that sealed their marriage would ever do.

And every time he had such thoughts, it only proved to him that he cared for this woman. *That* he feared more than anything else, when it came down to it.

But tonight there was no fear, only desire that swept him away and deposited him on a distant island where nothing else mattered except that his fingers brushed along the inside of her thigh until they found the wet folds of her pussy.

She arched up, pushing his fingers harder against her body and shuddering when he touched her slick, smooth clitoris and breached her core. He smiled, wicked, and invaded her even more deeply. He stroked her sex with his fingers, driving within her as she lifted her hips and squeezed the digits with her inner muscles.

He lowered his head and stroked his tongue against her sex, lapping up the sweet juices of her desire as she moaned out his name in a long, throaty gasp. How had he denied himself this for so many nights? He would certainly not make that mistake again.

He sucked her clitoris hard and her orgasm exploded in a rush of moans and a fluttering of hips and sex. She thrashed her head as her crisis built and finally crested and she relaxed back against his pillows.

She opened her eyes and looked at him, still flush with erotic release. She smiled, utterly wicked and somehow still in control, despite the fact that he had taken over her seduction and forced the first release of the night. Now that he looked at her, he realized it would not be the last. She was bent on proving to him how much he needed her and he was not about to reveal that he had already come to that very same conclusion.

She sat up and shifted to her knees before she placed her hands on his chest and laid him back against the bed. He lifted his hands behind his head as a pillow and chuckled as he looked at her.

"And what will you do now?" he teased.

But there was no teasing on her face or in her voice when she whispered, "Everything. Anything. Because you're mine."

Later, John knew he would pretend she had been in the thrill of the moment. Or that her words were just empty seduction. But in that moment, looking up at her, he knew what she meant and there was nothing empty about it. She was claiming him as her husband. Tonight, long before any vows would be said. She was giving him everything and asking him for the same in return. Tonight he would give it, even if he had misgivings about the future. Tonight, he *was* hers.

She dropped her mouth to his hard cock and began to suck him slowly, languidly, tasting him like she had all the time in the world to do so. Her tongue was a revelation, sending shockwaves of pleasure through his entire body and building him toward orgasm, only to back him off when it grew too close. She was an expert at pleasure and he surrendered himself to ministrations with a harsh, shuddering sigh as his inhibitions were swept away.

Mariah felt John give in to her and thrilled with the power she possessed. It might be temporary, yes, but for now it was hers and she intended to enjoy every moment. She nuzzled his cock, stroking it against her cheek before she drew him deep within her throat and sucked. His breath grew short and she rolled her tongue around him in slow, steady circles as he cried out in pleasure.

But it wasn't enough. She could make him come, of course, but she wanted to be closer. She released him, letting him fall from her lips with a wet pop and then she shimmied up his body, dragging hot kisses along his belly, his chest and finally his mouth, tangling their tongues together as she positioned her pussy over him and slowly lowered herself to take him deep within her.

He stretched her magnificently, filling her every inch, making her feel whole in ways she would never be able to express to him or anyone else. Their panting breaths merged into shared moans the further he disappeared into her willing body and finally he was seated fully inside.

She began to ride him, gripping his waist with her thighs and stroking in firm, repeated thrusts. He rubbed just perfectly against her clitoris and the pleasure she had felt when he licked her returned with equal power. Perhaps even more power since they were one body now, one joined entity reaching for a common goal of pleasure.

He lifted with more earnest desire and she felt him move as close to the edge as she was. She wanted them to fall together. To feel him pump within her just as she shivered in release. She pulled him to a seated position and wrapped her legs around his back as she rocked, never slowing, never giving either of them relief from her relentless need. He held her hips, guiding her restless movements until the pleasure was almost pain and she screamed out his name.

He growled with pleasure, the veins in his throat outlined as he pumped his hot seed deep within her. She took it all, milking him with her own release, their hips slamming together, their sweat merging as he kissed her so passionately that tears filled her eyes as she clung to him and wished, prayed that the moment would last forever.

Of course, it could not and did not. Pleasure faded and John collapsed back onto the bed, dragging her down across his chest as their panting breaths eased into something more normal and Mariah found she could speak once again.

"What meeting were you telling Mr. Thomason to prepare your waistcoat for?" she asked as she feathered soft kisses along his naked chest.

John shivered and she smiled. Oh yes, at least there would be this between them. Even if he didn't love her. Even if he never could. She would console herself with pleasure, it was all she could do.

"I received a note from my solicitor, Mr. Jacoby. The special license has been arranged. We marry in three days' time."

She stopped kissing him and stared up at him in what she knew was utter shock. "Th-three days?" she repeated. "So...so soon?"

He nodded, but he was watching her through a hooded and unreadable gaze. "Not so very soon. We agreed to marry a week ago, almost, and I have been bringing down the full force of my name and worth in order to bring this to pass quickly. It is the best way to protect you, after all."

"I knew you had been working diligently," she whispered. "But I simply did not realize—"

She cut herself off and he sighed softly.

"I will do my best to make you happy, Mariah," he said after they had both been silent for a long moment. "I can promise you nothing else but that."

She knew she should tell him it was enough, but the fact was that it wasn't. It wasn't enough. And she couldn't perceive a time when it would be.

CHAPTER 20

Adam entered the parlor and smiled as he found John in the seat he was uncomfortably perched in.

"I didn't expect to see you today," his brother said with true friendliness and welcome. "I hope you weren't kept waiting too long. I was in the middle of some business to do with the Clarke investment."

John blinked to clear the distraction that clouded his mind and managed to belatedly push to his feet.

"No, of course not. I knew you were likely busy. How are the arrangements advancing?"

His brother grinned. "Excellently. We should have a deal in place by day's end. I never knew how much I would enjoy shipping as an industry," he continued as he sat down and poured himself a cup of tea. "There is so much to learn."

Now when John smiled, he did not have to force the expression. He was truly happy for his brother as he began finding a place in the world that was beyond the scope of their father's influence. He knew full well how heady a prospect that could be. He remembered his own early days when he'd found his place, no matter how many years ago the same had happened to him.

"Did you come to talk to me about the work I have been doing in your company?" Adam asked as he wolfed down a biscuit in one bite. He cast his brother a quick glance. "I do hope I'm up to snuff."

"I have heard nothing but good about you from my foreman, I assure you," John said with a shrug. "No, the business is not what I'm here to talk about."

Adam sipped his tea and there was a shadow that crossed over his face that no one could deny. John frowned. His greatest hope was that his brother would one day shed the notion that he was constantly being judged, that he had something or someone to fear. Their father had pounded those facts into them as children and John hated feeling them, and seeing them on his brother's face.

"Then what is it that brings you here?" Adam finally asked very softly.

"It is...*happy* news," John said, forcing false brightness. "I am to marry in two days' time. On Saturday morning. At Helmsford Church near the park."

His brother nearly dropped his teacup and instead set it down with a clatter as he stared.

"M-Married?" he repeated and the word had emphasis, like it was foreign.

In truth, the entire idea felt foreign to John, though perhaps not in as negative a way as he had implied to Mariah a short time ago.

"Yes, married," he said, shaking his head and returning to the conversation rather than mull his thoughts.

"To whom?" his brother asked, but his voice was too quiet for his ignorance to be believed. Not when his eyes were bugged out and his face pale.

"To Mariah Desmond, of course." John waved a hand to dismiss any other possibility. "I wouldn't be fool enough to marry anyone else."

Adam blinked a few times in rapid succession. "You are marrying your mistress?"

"I am. Father is threatening her, which she does not deserve."

John dipped his head. "And this is the only way to fully protect her. With my money, my home and my name behind her, she will be at far lower risk."

His brother searched for a response, opening and shutting his mouth several times before he finally managed to find *something* to say. "There will be talk."

John laughed, but the sound was hollow. "Do you think so? She is not from any family even vaguely associated with rank, which would start tongues wagging anyway. And then there is the fact that I am marrying a woman who has been my lover for a short time and was, before that, my best friend's mistress for years. My best friend who died in so shocking a fashion that it is still openly discussed in ballrooms."

His brother pushed to his feet and staggered back, staring at John with such an expression that it forced John to his feet, as well. His brother looked…terrified.

"Y-You mean to tell me that Mariah was once the lover of Lord Heathcote?" he said, his voice trembling.

John nodded. "Owen, yes. You remember him, I'm sure. We were chums for years. I thought you knew the connection to Mariah?"

"I do remember him," his brother said on a gasp of breath. "I remember him well. But I did not realize…"

He spun on his heel and paced to the window where he stared outside, his shoulders taut and trembling. John moved toward him a step, then stopped. He wasn't certain his brother wanted him to pry, but wasn't this about him?

"Dear God, Adam, what is it?" he asked, trying to keep his tone light so the riotous emotions unexpectedly involved in this conversation would not be increased further.

His brother shook his head. "That was why he said—" He cut himself off.

"What?" John asked. "Who said what? What are you talking about?"

His brother turned, but there was almost no expression on his face. He was blank and pale.

"It isn't anything," he murmured. "I am simply very surprised by this turn of events, as I'm sure you have heard from dozens of people already."

John shook his head. "In truth, you are the first person to be told outside of Mariah's friend Vivien Manning."

His brother stared. "I am?"

"Yes. I came here today hoping you might stand up with me at the wedding on Saturday. It will be the smallest of affairs, but I'd like for you to be there."

"Why?" Adam whispered.

"Because you are my brother," John replied in surprise. "And I'm very happy to have you back in my life. There will be few who support any of this madness, but I think I can count on you to do so. Am I wrong?"

His brother swallowed hard. "No, you are not wrong. Of course I will stand up for you on Saturday."

"Excellent," John said as he moved forward to offer his brother a hand to shake. As Adam did so, he said, "I will send you something with all the details this afternoon. Now I must depart, I fear there is a great deal to be done in a short amount of time."

"Of course," his brother said as he led John to the door and into the foyer. As John took his hat, Adam stepped forward. "John—"

He said his name, but then cut it off so abruptly that John stared at him, as did the butler.

"Yes?" he asked.

"I—" his brother said. "That is—"

John wrinkled his brow at his brother's struggle. "What is it?"

"Nothing," Adam finally said with a shake of his head. "I will look for your missive today and be there for you Saturday."

John nodded and stepped outside, but as he mounted his horse, he could not help but be troubled by the nagging notion that his brother was more than shocked by John's sudden engagement or taken aback by his inclusion in what would likely be one of the most important days of John's life. He felt like Adam was hiding something.

And he just hoped that when he found out what it was, it wouldn't end up being a secret that would tear apart their delicate reunion.

~

"How can you want me to stand up for you at your wedding?" Vivien said, wincing as her fidgeting made the seamstress stab her with her needle.

The girl lifted her eyes in apology, but Vivien hardly seemed to notice. If Mariah hadn't been so out of sorts herself, she might have smiled at her normally cool friend's obvious nervousness.

"Because you are the dearest friend I have and I need all the support I can get," she said as she leaned back against the settee cushions and watched the seamstress continue her alteration of the gown Vivien would wear for Mariah's wedding in… Dear God, two days' time.

"But what a scene it will create," Vivien continued with a moan, "to have a woman seen as hardly better than a common whore stand up for you as you marry a man who is the grandson of a duke, for Christ's sake. I will make your situation far worse, not better."

Mariah stood and reached for her friend's hand. "Please, Vivien, don't argue with me about this. I do not think *anything* I ever do will result in my being accepted by those in the larger social sphere John moves in. And since he does not wish for this marriage to be real in any way, the best I can hope for is that I will still have my true friends to surround me."

Vivien stared at her and the anxiety that had lined her face faded. "Of course, this is *your* day. I did not mean to place my own worries on to you when you already have a great deal to fret over. I'm sorry."

Mariah released Vivien's hand and shook her head. "No, there is to be none of that. No apologies."

Vivien watched her as she retook her seat. "What of your gown?"

She sighed. "John has paid some exorbitant sum for it to be ready Friday night. I believe there are five seamstresses sewing madly on it now." She stared at a point far across the room without seeing it. "It is ridiculous for him to do so, but he seems to want me to have some sort of passable wedding, as if this were all real."

Vivien pursed her lips. "But it is real for you, isn't it?"

"If you mean I shall marry a man I love, then certainly it is more real than anything I have ever known." She shook her head. "But it is meaningless nonetheless. John wishes to protect me and this is the only way he can see to do so."

"At least that is romantic," her friend said.

Mariah stared at her. "A less romantic notion I have never known. He would *protect* a dog that was being kicked on the street, too. No, this resolution speaks more to his character rather than anything to do with me."

"Then things are still difficult between you?" Vivien asked.

Mariah took a peek at the seamstress. She had slipped across the room to record some measurements in a little book, so Mariah edged closer and whispered, "He has begun making love to me again, at least."

Vivien smiled. "Then I think all this proves he *does* care for you, Mariah."

Mariah's heart leapt, just as it did any time she allowed that fleeting thought to cross her exhausted mind. But she pushed it away.

"He may care, but that does not mean he loves. I shall accept the first, but I do not think I shall ever stop longing for the second. And that will mean a great deal of heartache, I fear." She smiled. "But then, it will not be much different from many other marriages in Upper Society, will it?"

"I suppose not," Vivien said, then pursed her lips as the seamstress returned and they were no longer at liberty to speak of more intimate subjects.

Mariah was just as pleased for the shift in conversation. She had to accept that in two days time she would be the wife of a man she loved, but would not, or could not, love her in return. Those were the facts.

And someday, perhaps she would find a way to endure them with the grace befitting her new station in life.

CHAPTER 21

Mariah stared at the clock with increasing frustration and anxiety tightening her chest. It had been fifteen minutes since her lady's maid had left to find a bit of ribbon to wind through her hair and there was no sign of the girl's return yet.

Mariah stood with a huff of her breath and moved toward the bell. She had rung it once already with no response. If she didn't know the servants so well, she might think they were ignoring her on purpose, as some kind of sign of their disapproval. But they had been nothing but kind, both in and out of John's presence, so she doubted it was that.

Something was keeping Nellie from her side.

She went to the door and opened it, peeking into the hallway. It was silent. Of course, many of the servants had already left for the church, where they would stand in the wings to watch as John pledged his life to hers. But there were a few to stay behind and ready the wedding luncheon and help see her off.

But not a one appeared. She didn't even hear them bustling about.

"Hello?" she called into the hallway. "Swanson? Nellie? Gregory?"

Silence remained her only companion and she stepped into the hallway and moved down to the stairs at the end of the walkway.

"Is anyone here?"

Nothing.

She walked down the stairs at a fast clip, with every intention of entering the downstairs area that housed the kitchens and the servant areas. But before she could reach the backstair, the door to the parlor opened and a man she did not recognize stepped into her path.

She flinched as she looked up at him. He was very tall, with graying hair and a hawkish nose that he looked down with a sniff of disapproval.

"O-oh!" she stammered as she took an instinctive step backward. "I didn't realize there was a visitor in the house."

Perhaps this caller was the reason for the absence of the servants. This man, with his icy-cold demeanor, could certainly hold sway over the maids and footmen with no trouble. And if Swanson knew him…

"You must be Mariah," the man said, his tone dark and unfriendly as he looked her up and down. "I was in a hurry the last time we met, but now I see why he fucks you."

Mariah staggered back until her bottom collided with a table along the hallway. Certainly she was no stranger to such strong language, but she was not accustomed to men directing it toward her with little regard to her gender or her new position in life.

"I beg your pardon?" she said, outrage in her voice.

He smiled. "Oh please, save your little show for John. He appreciates it, I suppose, but I do not. Though I could…" He trailed off and leered at her. "Mmm."

She lifted her chin as he undressed her with his eyes. It was a decidedly unpleasant feeling, especially when she was standing before him in her wedding dress.

"Who are you, sir? What are you doing here?"

"Don't you know?" he laughed. "Oh, I suppose you would not.

The boy does not exactly display portraits of me about the parlor, does he?"

Mariah swallowed as she took a second look at the man. Now she saw a glimpse of John here. A hint of him there. And she knew. But she still whispered, "Who are you?"

"I am to be your father-in-law," he said as he moved on her. "Or I would be, *if* I was going to allow for this farce of a marriage to proceed."

She looked again, into those eyes. And realized they were the same as the man in the mask who had attacked her.

"You," she breathed.

He smiled. "We meet again."

Mariah turned to run. It was her only thought, escape. But the man she now knew to be Vaughn Rycroft was faster and caught her by the arm in a grip so steely that she feared he might break her bones in two as he hauled her into the parlor from which he had emerged.

She tugged against him but was no match to his superior strength. He threw her into a settee and kicked the door shut behind him. She looked around and drew back as she realized they were not alone. One of the guards John had hired to protect her was standing in the corner of the room, arms folded, as he stared at her.

She knew in that moment that the guard was not going to help her. Clearly he had been reached by Vaughn Rycroft. Paid more money to betray her than John had paid for his protection. But she had to try to save herself, it was all she knew to do.

"Please," she begged the guard without shame. "This is the man my fiancé hired you to protect me from."

The man sneered and looked at Rycroft instead. "Want me to check on the others?"

"Yes." Rycroft looked toward the side door of the chamber. "I doubt they're having any trouble, but best to be certain."

The guard nodded and left through the side door. She heard his heavy footfalls as he moved toward the servant area and her heart lodged in her chest.

"What did you do to them?" she asked, her voice cracking.

Rycroft looked at her with a smile of pure wicked amusement. "You are worried about the servants? How quaint of you."

She firmed her jaw and glared at him. "What did you do?"

"Nothing." He shrugged. "Yet, at least. Watching the one guard on duty who I did not own be killed put them in line immediately. They are tied up now and quite malleable, I assure you."

Mariah swallowed a scream. The other guard...dead. The servants, forced to watch in terror and then tied up to wait for their fate. And all because of this man. All because of *her*.

Fear reared inside of her, as wild as an untrained stallion, but she fought to tame it. This was the time for calm, not hysterics. She owed herself and the others in the house that composure.

"I am a reasonable woman, you know," she said, wishing her voice did not tremble. "We can talk about this, come to an arrangement that would be mutually beneficial."

Rycroft had been fiddling with a decanter on the sideboard as she battled to control her reaction and he turned toward her now with an ugly chuckle

"That may be true, but I fear the time for discussion is over, my dear. Had I known you would end up being a far greater thorn in my side, I would have ensured you died in that fire with your former lover. But now I have a better idea."

Mariah stared. "What are you talking about?"

He glared at her. "Please do not go stupid on me now, my dear. You were only just becoming interesting. You know I'm speaking of your former lover, the Earl of Heathcote. Unless you have others who have died in fires over the years?"

She squeezed her eyes shut as images bombarded her. "You are saying that *you* set the fire which killed Owen?"

"And understanding dawns," Rycroft laughed. "I *arranged* for the fire, yes."

Bile flooded Mariah's mouth, but she swallowed it back. What he said might not be true. It could very well be a ploy to frighten her into acquiescence.

"Why should I believe your lies?" she asked, lifting her chin in defiance. "Why would you do such a thing?"

Rycroft shrugged. "Owen was a friend to my son. One who was encouraging him to continue his severing of ties with me. I tried to turn the earl to my side, but he refused to betray John." He shook his head in disgust. "I had no choice but to end him, in order to keep him from doing even more damage. John *will* be under my thumb again. I can assure you."

Mariah staggered back. Memories were beginning to return. Discussion that had seemed meaningless at the time, but now became most important played in her head. Owen had spoken of some kind of trouble regarding John before his death. His explanation to her then had been so vague, but now she could see how his concerns must have had to do with Vaughn Rycroft.

"You burned him alive in his bed," she whimpered as she tried not to think of Owen's suffering.

"I did, indeed." Rycroft shrugged. "In battle they call that collateral damage, I believe. Unfortunately, *you* must be the same."

Mariah tried to maintain her decorum. She tried not to lose herself to terror and heartbreak. But it was impossible. Her voice was out of her control and as she sank from the settee to the floor, she heard her screams echo in the quiet room around her.

No one else would hear them. No one who could help her. Or help John. Or stop whatever madness this man had planned for her before her wedding day was over.

~

John paced at the front of the church, unable to keep himself from looking over at the front door anytime there was even a creak of the old building.

"Is it possible, Mr. Rycroft, that the young lady is not coming?" the vicar asked, in as kind a tone as he could muster through his own frustration over his wasted time.

John turned on him with a scowl. He was thinking the very same thing, of course, but hearing it from someone else's lips made him angry.

"She would not change her mind without speaking to me," he hissed. "She would not be that unkind."

That much, at least, was true. He could very well imagine Mariah refusing to marry him at the last minute. She had been hesitant about this arrangement from the first moment and never kept those hesitations a secret. But to leave him standing at the altar like a fool with his brother, three-quarters of his servants and a spattering of church-related strangers watching him did not seem to be something she would willingly choose to do.

Especially since when he left her that morning, she was readying herself for the wedding. She'd had ample opportunity to change her mind to his face.

The vicar gave him a smile filled with disbelief and stepped back to whisper with an altar attendant. As the man left earshot, John leaned toward his brother.

"Where could she be?" he asked through clenched teeth. "She is nearly half an hour late and that isn't in her nature. Am I merely an idiot not to see that she has run off rather than marry me?"

His brother shifted and his face reddened as he stared at his boots. John pursed his lips.

"What is wrong with you, Adam? You have been odd all day. I don't think I've had two words put together from you. Are you in such disapproval of my choice, because you, like Mariah, had ample time to speak your worries before today."

Adam shook his head. "No, it isn't that. Not at all."

"Then what?" John snapped and his voice echoed in the quiet church so that every eye in the place swiveled on him in something akin to pity. He lowered his tone and repeated, "Then what?"

Adam sucked in a breath. "I just...it's about *him*..." He stopped and shook his head. "No, I shouldn't. I'm sorry."

But it was too late to drop the subject now. John stared at his brother.

"*Him*? There is only one *him* in our lives. Are you saying you know something about our father? Something that has put you this out of sorts?"

His brother swallowed with what looked to be considerable difficulty, then opened and shut his mouth like a fish. John moved forward and caught his lapels, hauling him closer.

"What is going on? You tell me now!" he shouted and this time he didn't care if he made the entire church uncomfortable with his emotions.

His brother shoved back and staggered free into the aisle of the church. As he smoothed his lapels, he choked out, "Father has wanted you back under his control for years. Especially once he realized you were making a name and a fortune for yourself. He thought one way to obtain that control was to use your friends against you. He turned to the Earl of Heathcote, as he was your closest friend."

John drew back and shook his head in confusion. "Owen? When did he speak to Owen?"

"For a few months before his...death, Father called on him mercilessly, trying every method of bribery, extortion and threat to turn him to a spy. But Heathcote was too good a friend to you. He refused, even though Father insisted. Finally, he grew tired of Father's interference and said he was going to you with every detail of Father's attempt."

"Why hadn't he come to me from the beginning?" John asked with a shake of his head. "I could have nipped that annoyance in the bud."

"He said that knowing the lengths Father would go to would hurt you." Adam dipped his chin. "He was, I believe, trying to protect you."

John bit back a sound of pain. He had spent the past few months with dark feelings for Owen. His friend's treatment of Mariah had been a bone of contention between them long before and even since his death. But here his friend had been trying to protect him all along. Being more the family member to him than anyone else had ever been.

"But you know Father. He realized he had gone too far. A bad word from Owen would be even more powerful than a good one could have been. He went...mad with fury." His brother hesitated. "And he plotted to kill your friend, in the most painful way possible."

John's lips parted as what his brother was not saying became as clear as what he had.

"You cannot be implying that our father caused the fire that burned my best friend alive."

Adam nodded. "Y-Yes."

John staggered beneath the weight of this confession. And as the layers of it sank in, he stared at his brother with new and fresh betrayal.

"Wait, how do you know this? *When* did you know this?"

"From the beginning," his brother whispered. "He took me along on every meeting with Owen. And he...he asked me to arrange the fire."

"Did you?" John asked, his voice as hollow as his heart in that moment. "Did you kill my best friend?"

"No!" his brother cried. "I didn't. I couldn't do that. When I refused, he hired someone else."

"Yet you knew his plans and did nothing to warn Owen." John clenched his fists. "So in a way you did kill him."

"Yes," his brother said as he covered his eyes and let out a low sound of pain. "I did. And I have hardly slept or eaten since that night for the guilt."

"And yet you were willing to come and play me for a fool. To betray me the way my friend would not." John moved on him.

"Admit it, you came to me with your sad story of being cut off in order to play spy for our father."

"Yes," Adam admitted. "I did at the beginning. But the more we talked, the more I was free of him, I knew my actions were wrong. I began to tell him only half-truths. Lies when I could manage them. But he quickly guessed at my deception and instead he bought into a few of the guards you hired to protect Mariah."

John shook his head. "He owns some of my guards?" he whispered, his anger at his brother, his grief at his part in his friend's death, fading in the face of this news.

His brother nodded. "Including the one who I believe is with Mariah today. And…and that may be why she is late to the wedding, John."

For a moment, everything in John's world froze. He no longer heard the bustling of the vicar and his people, the echoes in the church, he no longer saw the scene around him…even his brother. All he could think about was Mariah, caught in a web his father had designed. His father who had resorted to murder once. And a horrible murder at that.

There was no doubt he would do so again, if he thought it would lead to control over John…or even just as a punishment to him for refusing to bend to his father's will.

"John—" His brother began, reaching for him.

John jerked away. "Don't touch me. I have nothing to say to you. Not now. Now I must focus on her. I must get to her," he gasped as he began to run for the doors.

"Then I'm coming with you," Adam said, following on his heels even though John could hardly bring himself to look at him.

"Vicar Mosley, please call for the Watch to be sent to my home."

The vicar was asking questions, but John ignored him. At the back of the church, he found his servants gathered, staring at him with gazes of concern, even though they had not overheard any of his conversation with his brother.

"Ladies, you must stay here, I fear the house is not safe," he said with a quick glance over them. "And I realize, gentleman, that your duty is not to put yourselves in harm's way for me, but I believe there is a credible threat against Miss Mariah and the other servants who stayed behind to assist her. If any of you would be willing to follow me to the household and investigate, I would truly appreciate it. Though I cannot guarantee what we will walk into there."

There was a moment where the servants glanced at each other, then several of the footmen and grooms moved forward.

"We'll help, sir," the first footman, Lysinrig, said. "We came in one of the lower carriages and will follow in it straightaway."

John did not wait for more answer than that, but rushed outside. The wedding carriage was to escort Mariah from the house here, so his horse was waiting for him outside rather than a rig. Just as well, for he was faster. John did not address the man holding its reins, but swung up and took off without even waiting for Adam to mount and do the same.

All he could think about was Mariah. And pray that she had not come to harm at the hands of the devil disguised as his father.

CHAPTER 22

John brought his horse to a short stop on the drive at his home and he threw himself down. He raced for the door without any thought of anything but Mariah. Her name had been a part of his heartbeat all the way here and his mind had been bombarded with so many images of her that he could hardly think now. But think he must, for the danger to her…the danger to them all…was now at its peak.

He reached the door and stepped to the side, drawing in a breath before he reached for the handle and turned. It swung inward and he hesitated, uncertain if he would be greeted by a shot from a pistol, a billy club to the head or just a scene of carnage that included the woman he—

Well, the woman he intended to marry.

And of course he was unarmed no matter what awaited him. He did not normally carry a weapon on his person, as some men did. Something he intended to remedy if he survived this awful day.

But no sound broke the silence of his foyer and slowly John peered into the quiet house. What he saw made the blood drain from his face. Broken glass littered the foyer carpet and the picture that had once hung there was cockeyed and torn from a struggle of some kind. There were a few drops of blood staining the floor and a streak on the wall.

His heart sank.

"John," his brother panted as he skidded inside the foyer with him. Adam looked around. "Dear God."

"Yes," John murmured as he eased inside. "We can only hope there *is* a God and that He has been kind to us today."

He motioned his brother to the other side of the door and looked back. The servants with their carriage had likely been slowed by the traffic on the London streets this sunny Saturday morning, but John couldn't wait for their assistance. He had to know what was awaiting him inside.

He moved inside the foyer and peered into the first parlor, but it was empty. Adam did the same on the other side of the hallway, with much the same results.

"Some broken items," he said softly. "But no one in residence."

"Damn this," John said and then called out. "Who is here? I demand you show yourself at once."

There were creaks and sounds from the short set of stairs that led down into the kitchens and public servant areas and then the door opened. John steadied himself, but it wasn't an attacker who greeted him.

It was Vivien Manning, with a pistol pointed at his heart. When she saw it was him, the pistol lowered and her pale face, complete with a large bruise and dried blood caked on her forehead, relaxed.

"Thank God you called out," she said as she held out the pistol to him with a shaking head. "If you had come downstairs without warning, I might have shot you."

"Vivien?" he cried as he snatched the pistol from her and shoved it into his waistband. "What in the world?"

She shrugged. "I came to retrieve Mariah and ride with her to the church as arranged. What I found instead was a madman bent on removing her."

"Our father," Adam said and John flinched at his voice. Adam, who could have prevented all this if not for his cowardice.

Vivien nodded as her gaze darted from one brother to the other. "I'm afraid that is so. We struggled in the foyer and he struck me in the head with the butt of a pistol. When I woke a few moments later, he was gone with her."

John dipped his head. "Jesus. But she was living, still?"

"She was," Vivien said. "And willing to fight in order to escape, but with his men and his size outweighing hers, she had no hope of that, I fear. As to where he took her, I am not sure, but before we sort that out, I think you had best come down to the servant area."

John hesitated. His first reaction was to burst from the house and out into the street to find his father and Mariah. But that was not logical. He had no place to begin that search. And he owed it to his servants, who were as innocent victims of this madness as anyone, to check in on them.

He followed Vivien into the lower rooms of the house and as he entered the kitchen, he drew back. Swanson's arm was bound to his side by a sling fashioned from someone's torn shirt. Still, he tended to Mariah's lady's maid, wiping blood from her swollen lip with a dishcloth. On the floor, covered with a sheet, was a body.

"Dear God," he murmured. "Who is that?"

Swanson looked up at his voice and relief came to his expression. "Thank God you are all right, sir. That, I fear, is Mr. Westinghouse, one of Miss Mariah's guards. He died trying to protect her from the other one…the blackguard who was in league with your father. He did fight valiantly."

"Something that will be of little comfort to his family," John said with a shake of his head. "Now I must ask you, did any of you have any idea where my father might have taken Mariah? Anything the other guard said or my father himself, or any of his other men?"

Swanson shook his head. "I made those inquiries already, sir. No one heard or saw anything that I think could be of help in your search."

"I might know something. Something I wish I didn't," Vivien said, her tone shaken and more emotional than anything John had ever heard from her.

He turned on her. "What is it?"

"Your father...I have sometimes heard his name associated with...the sale of women into sexual servitude to important men abroad on the Continent and beyond. It is whispered in our circles that it is a side business of his that brings him money and prestige." She wrinkled her nose in disgust. "I—I never told you, John. I should have, God, I should have."

John shook his head. "It seems everyone's attempts to protect me from the true nature of my father have only resulted in more trouble for us all. He—he murdered Owen."

Vivien collapsed into the nearest chair and stared up at him. "No."

"Yes, I am afraid he did," Adam said, his voice choked. "And this *side business*, as Miss Manning puts it, is very true. Though I think he does it for pleasure as much as business. Controlling others, as you well know, brother, is a bit of a hobby of our father's."

"Why would he do that, though? Why not just kill Mariah?" John said, almost unable to voice that final question.

"Come, John," Adam said, and he looked John in the eye for the first time since he had admitted his part in this scheme. "He wants you under his thumb. If she is dead, he cannot use her as a pawn. Send her off to some unknown and horrible fate and you would hold out hope that you could still save her. He will spend years giving you false hope of finding her, all while using your love for her to keep you in line."

John swallowed. His love for her. Something he had been denying almost since the first moment he clapped eyes on her three years before. And yet there it was, stated so simply by a brother who had betrayed him.

"You are very correct, I think," he choked out. "But these

arrangements must take time. Even if he had already intended to sell Mariah out from under me, she would have to be taken to a ship and loaded. How long ago did they leave, Vivien?"

She glanced at the clock. "Within the hour. No more than that."

"Then we have time." He turned on Adam. "Which docks does Father use for most of his transactions?"

Adam shook his head. "They won't let you pass. But they will allow me. You must take me with you."

John stared. "And how could I trust *you* after everything you have confessed today?"

His brother pursed his lips. "You cannot. But if you wish to find Mariah, I may be your only hope. I will either redeem myself or I could die trying. At least we would have tried to save Mariah, at least you will know that I tried to help."

John blinked. "I suppose you are right. Then let us obtain some weapons from my offices and go. Mariah's life hangs in the balance. We have no time to lose."

Mariah perched on the very edge of the uncomfortable wooden chair in the reeking hold of a ship, listening as her fate was bartered over like she was cattle.

"Her red hair alone will be worth a great deal," Vaughn Rycroft said. "I've had inquiries from one of Napoleon's lackeys in the last week alone. To give me less than ten thousand is a mockery."

The ship captain shrugged. "I might be able to get ten thousand for her, yes. But I can't give you the full amount. I've never given you more than half as a finder's fee, Rycroft, so let's not be foolish."

Rycroft sighed, utterly put upon. "Fine. Send it along to me tomorrow. Oh, and, Captain, do tell your men to go easy on her on the way across. If there's nothing left, no one will buy her."

The captain showed a toothless grin and leaned over to smell

Mariah's hair. She shut her eyes and tried to make her mind blank. She was not this body. Whatever happened to it was not happening to her.

It didn't really work, but somehow she kept herself from screaming as she had in John's home and continued to do when Rycroft struck Vivien down. She could only pray her friend was all right.

Otherwise, she doubted any of her other prayers would be answered.

"I don't know, Rycroft," the captain said. "This one will be hard not to use up. But we'll do our best."

He got up and laughed his way from the room. When he was gone, Mariah opened her eyes and stared evenly at Rycroft.

"I thought you looked like John when I first saw you," she said quietly. "But you are nothing like him. The fact that you could sire such an honorable and good man is nothing short of a miracle."

Rycroft shrugged. "We all have our weaknesses. But John will come under my control soon enough."

"How can you assume that?" she scoffed, wishing she could rub where the ropes were cutting into her wrists. It was highly uncomfortable.

"If he believes someday he might be able to get you back, he will do anything."

Mariah shook her head and tried not to picture John's desperation.

"Why would he want to find me? After all, as you have reminded me the entire way to these docks and through your negotiations, I am nothing more than a whore. His marriage to me was a whim at best. If I am not his responsibility, he will soon forget me."

She didn't believe those words for a moment, but she would not give Rycroft the reward of her heartbreak. Or her fear.

"Hm, perhaps that is the way it should be, but you see, I believe he fancies himself in love with you. Either way, he isn't the sort of man to leave you to your fate, is he?" Rycroft smiled. "And if he won't turn to me, I will have punished him thoroughly for his refusal. He will at least think twice before he does such a thing again."

Mariah swallowed back a swell of bile that rose to her throat. "Are we finished here, Mr. Rycroft?" she asked. "I would very much like you to leave."

He laughed as he pushed from his place and looked down at her. "Soon I'll be the least villainous person you know, my dear. Enjoy your passage, I'm sure it will be eventful."

Mariah pinched her lips together to keep them from trembling and silently wished for John. Prayed for him to arrive and save her, even though she knew there was very little chance of that.

Except, as Rycroft headed for the stairs that led up to the deck of the ship, there was a commotion. And she knew, as well as she knew the beating of her own heart, that John was there.

The Watch had met them just as they departed the house, so overcoming the ship with eight armed men, six of them with official papers, was far easier than John would have ever imagined. Most of the sailors simply followed orders. They were no masterminds and they folded when faced with officials.

It didn't stop him from wanting to wring their necks as the guard officers pushed them back into a waiting crowd for questioning on what they were calling "the matter".

The matter. Mariah was not a matter, she was a woman. A woman he loved and could very well lose, if he hadn't already lost her. His stomach turned.

"When will we move into the ship?" he demanded to the guard leader.

The man looked at him with annoyance. "In a moment, sir. Please, allow us to do our job."

John stepped away, but his acquiescence was for show alone. He wasn't about to abandon Mariah to the inept investigation of the guard. He shot a look at his brother.

Adam straightened up and motioned toward the ship just across a thin plank in the distance. The *Lusty Maiden*, it was called, a moniker that made John sick when he thought of its captive cargo.

"Distract them, yes?" he said softly. "While I board."

Adam tensed. "By yourself?"

He nodded. "I'm armed. And I know what I'm facing, probably better than these men."

After a hesitation, his brother said, "Is there anything I can do to dissuade you?"

"No. This is my future wife. My best and truest friend. My life." He shuddered. "I would leave her safety to no other man."

Adam pondered for a moment, then nodded. "Then best go while the sailors are a bit rowdy."

John looked at the restless crowd. A few of the sailors had begun to argue with the guard. No one was even looking toward the ship yet, so he drew his pistol and headed up the plank and toward the captain's quarters.

Mariah staggered as Rycroft dragged her to her feet and peered through the gaps in the wooden cabin toward the loud noises outside. For the first time since he'd taken her, he looked less than smugly satisfied. If he weren't holding a knife to her throat, she might have enjoyed that more.

"Bollocks," he cursed against her ear. "It appears Adam has involved himself in this mess, despite my orders to keep his mouth shut and do as he was told. That is the only way John could have found us so quickly."

Mariah's heart leapt with joy, but it was tempered by worry. The man who held her was a madman, but a calculating one. She had known men like him before, though not to this extreme. If they could not have what they wanted, no one else would. Which meant John was in as much danger as she was if he burst into this room in an attempt to save her.

Did he know that? Was he acquainted enough with his father's true self to protect himself? Or would his feelings and connection to her blind him?

"Kill me," she said, tensing as she spoke the words.

Rycroft glanced down at her in true shock. "I beg your pardon?"

"Kill me. It will distract him enough that you can escape. Isn't that what you want?" She shivered even as the words fell from her lips.

"You *do* love him, don't you?" Rycroft asked. "You're ready to sacrifice yourself for him. What a weakness."

The door slowly opened before he could say more and John's tall, broadshouldered body blocked the sun from outside as he stepped into the cramped quarters.

"A weakness in your eyes," he said as he held a pistol steady on his father. "But I've never shared your opinion on much, including that. As for you…" His gaze flitted to her and she saw his relief that she was whole. "There will be no noble sacrifices today, my dear."

Mariah swallowed and felt the knife press to her skin as her throat worked. John might not be right about the second part of his statement, but she would keep that to herself at present.

"Your brother betrayed me in the end, eh?" Rycroft said with a shake of his head. "That boy is a fool."

"That *boy* did everything you wanted. You destroyed him." John clenched his teeth. "I'm not certain he will ever be whole again. But this isn't about him. At least not entirely. Why don't you let Mariah go and we'll see if we can come to terms?"

Rycroft laughed, but the sound was highly unpleasant. "Terms? No, that time is over. I tried to come to terms with you weeks ago and you spat in my face. The only language you understand is that of loss. I should have remembered that from your mother. If you are threatened by loss, you respond positively. So I will take what you hold most dear."

Mariah shook as the knife blade cut just a touch into her skin and stared at John with wide eyes. His breath went short and he paled.

"You have no cards now," John said, his voice deceptively calm. "You *know* that. You played your hand and you've lost. Let Mariah go and I might…" His mouth pinched and Mariah could see how little he wanted to say the next words. "I could still protect you from the worst of the consequences of these actions."

"You protect me?" His father laughed. "No, I doubt that."

Mariah could feel Rycroft's agitation growing with each passing moment. The knife shook against her skin, nicking her here and there as he lost concentration and looked at the door behind John.

"I think you may be right that my cards are played out," he said and his voice shook a little at her ear. "But if I must lose, John, then I'm afraid I cannot allow you to win."

The world seemed to shift into half-time. The knife cut into Mariah's skin and she cried out at the pain. John cursed, though she would never remember what word he said exactly, and suddenly there was a plume of smoke curling out from the gun he had fired. Her ears rang with the explosiveness of it and she squeezed her eyes shut and waited to feel the dual burning pains of her throat being slashed and the bullet striking her.

Instead the weight of Vaughn Rycroft's grip released from her arm and fell away behind her. The knife slid against her skin, but with no force, causing a minor, stinging scratch as the weapon clattered to one side.

She staggered forward and into John's arms, where he held her tightly against his chest and tried to pull her away from the death behind her. But she had to look.

Vaughn Rycroft had a bullet hole squarely between his eyes. He stared up at the ceiling as a pool of blood collected beneath him, his gaze empty.

"Come away," John said, turning her toward the door. "Come away, my love."

CHAPTER 23

Mariah stepped into the master bedroom of John's home a few hours later to find him sitting in the settee before the dying fire. He stared at the drink in his hand without taking a sip. She winced at his expression—hollow, empty, broken.

"John?" she whispered.

He jerked his gaze at her with a gasp of surprise and then smiled, trying to hide his emotions, to protect her, though she was no longer the one who needed it.

"I'm sorry. I promised to return to the parlor, but I sat down and lost track of time." He moved to stand. "I'm certain the Watch still has a plethora of questions."

Mariah shook her head and motioned him to remain where he was. "The guard has departed in its entirety. Your brother has somehow handled it all. Though I think there was enough evidence that they would have come to the proper conclusion even without Adam's interference."

"He said he would redeem himself or die trying," John muttered. "But he isn't the one who lies dead, is he?"

"Do you blame yourself for that?" she whispered as she moved on him slowly.

"Of course," he said as he set his drink down on the floor, as if he didn't care where it went. "I am the one who fired the bullet into the man's brain."

"And I suppose you blame me, as well?" she whispered.

He jerked his gaze to hers. "Don't be foolish, of course I don't. You were my father's victim, having done no more wrong than being someone I care for."

She stared at him. That was more of an admission of feelings than he had ever shared with her. It was not enough, but it still warmed her even though she did not wish it to.

"You *must* blame me if you blame yourself, for *you* are a victim as much as I am." She sat down beside him. "You did not ask to be born Rycroft's son. Nor to be used by him as a pawn in any of his twisted schemes. You came to that ship in order to save me from his wicked plan. And that you did. I know that if you could have avoided spilling even a drop of his blood you would have."

"Yes," he mused. "But why? Why do I feel such guilt, such heart-break over his death? He was a sick, controlling bastard who destroyed all he touched with a glee that far surpassed the bound-aries of madness. He was a dog who needed to be put down. Yet I grieve."

"Because he was your father," she soothed. "And that means something to a good man. Like you."

He glanced over at her. "I hope you know I do not regret saving you, Mariah."

She nodded without hesitation. She might know little else, but that was plain. "Of course."

"I regret you were ever put in that position, but if the same choices were placed before me now, I would end it the same way." He reached out and touched the place where her neck had been bandaged. "Perhaps I would have fired sooner."

She covered his fingers and smiled. "John, you have spent the past few weeks tending to me. Whether it was my physical desires or my wellbeing, you have not thought once of yourself."

"A few times I have," he said with a smile that warmed her. He could still seduce, which gave her hope for his recovery when she was gone.

"You know what I mean. Please allow me to take care of you now." She leaned forward and brushed her lips to his. "Please, let me take away some of the ugliness of today and replace it with good."

He nodded as he lifted her onto his lap. She kissed him, tracing his tongue with her own, tasting him, sucking him, feeling him relax into her touch the way he deserved to do after today. She massaged his shoulders as he leaned back against the settee and was rewarded by the feel of his hardening erection against her thigh.

He groaned as she pulled away from his kiss and stared down at him in the firelight. They did not speak, but neither of them looked away as she stood up and stripped out of her gown to stand before him naked. He lifted his hips and removed his trousers but never got to his shirt because she straddled him as soon as his cock was naked and speared herself down over him in one heated thrust.

"Great God," he groaned out.

She smiled as she began to rock her hips. Each thrust was slow and seductive, building the pleasure of the joining in inches rather than miles. They might not have forever anymore, but they had the whole night and she was in no rush to bring their joining to an end.

He lifted his hips to hasten what she would not, lifting her almost off the settee in his enthusiasm to drive deeper, to claim faster, and the edge on which she teetered rapidly became too unsteady. She found herself falling into orgasm, deep and slow, that rocked her as she continued to ride him, ride him, ride him.

"There is nothing better than seeing you come," he growled and then his face contorted with pleasure and he burst within her, filling her with his essence until they collapsed together, arms around each other, breath matched in pants.

She held him for a long time, smoothing her hands along his back as she rested her head in the crook of his shoulder and appreciated the way their bodies were still joined, their heartbeats matched.

He sighed and the painful sound broke the spell. "I shall need to speak to the vicar tomorrow about rescheduling the wedding. I would think we could repeat this next weekend, though hopefully with less high drama."

She drew back and stared at him. He seemed utterly serious. With a gasp, she got to her feet and lifted her chemise up to cover herself.

"John, we shall not marry now."

He stared at her. "What? Of course we will."

"No. We will not." She drew the chemise over her head and folded her arms. "I do appreciate your continued attempts to make this right, but the reason you were marrying me was that you felt it was imperative to protect me from your father. Now that the threat is gone there is no need for me to be your wife. I cannot fulfill that place."

He stared at her. "Do you say this because of what my father tried to do to you today?"

She stepped toward him before she could stop herself. "No. I could no more judge you for his actions than I would judge anyone else in this house. John—" She cut herself off and then sat down next to him. She took his hand and forced herself to look into his eyes. "John, I cannot marry you because I love you."

He jolted and she forced herself not to look away from him in embarrassment.

"I don't understand how such an emotion should make a marriage less palatable," he said, his voice unreadable. "I would think it would make you desire such a union between us all the more."

She forced a smile. "Almost dying today made me want to live. It made me want a future. But with you...with you there would be no future. What you have proposed would become a prison to us both. To you because you do not love me and to me because I do."

He stared at her. "And that is your only reason for refusal?"

She nodded. "Yes, of course."

"And what if I could offer you a future, rather than a prison?"

She stared at him. His handsome face was virtually unreadable and she struggled to decide if he was serious or not.

"How could you do that?" she asked. "I doubt either of us could change our feelings."

"No," he admitted and her heart sank. "My feelings are set in stone, I'm afraid. But I can tell you they are not what you believe them to be."

"I—I don't understand," she said, unable to bring her voice to a level above a scant whisper.

"No, I have made sure of that over the past few weeks, hell, over the past few years. But I want to correct that. I…" He hesitated. "I love you, Mariah."

Her mouth dropped open and she stared at him. She was dreaming. Except when she pinched herself, she remained just where she was, only with a sore spot tingling her arm.

"I do want a wife," he continued. "To protect me as much as I protect her. To be a partner. A friend. A lover. That wife is you. It could only ever be you."

She rose to her feet and backed away, still uncertain that what was happening was real. "Please don't say these things if you do not mean them. It will only make everything worse in the end."

"I mean what I say," he promised as he got up and wrapped his arms around her waist. "You should know that to be true, if nothing else. I love you. I shall love you until the end of my days. And I want to marry you. *Now*."

She stared at him. There was nothing disingenuous about what he said. He looked her straight in the eye. And in his face she saw something she never would have expected or hoped for.

She saw love. Love for her. Hope for their future.

She cupped his cheeks. "When did this happen?"

He laughed. "I have been trying to track that very answer," he said. "And I believe I fell in love with you the first moment I saw you. I was only too daft, too stubborn to admit it. But now that I have, I wish to scream it from the rooftops, to announce it in the middle of the street. But you have not yet answered my question."

"Your question," she repeated, still stricken by this shocking turn.

"Marry me," he repeated gently.

"I will," she whispered. "I will very happily."

And he leaned down to kiss her and swept her away.

READ AN EXCERPT FROM HER PERFECT MATCH

BOOK 3 OF THE MISTRESS MATCHMAKER SERIES

"I'm tired," she whispered instead.

Rachel handed her the soap. "Oh, and why wouldn't you be? You hardly had any sleep. Perhaps the bath will help you relax and—"

"No," she said as she lathered the soap in her hands absently. "Not physically tired. Something deeper. I'm *tired* of being the most celebrated mistress in Society. I'm tired of hosting fetes and pleasure parties."

Rachel pursed her lips. "You have done so for so long. Who could blame you for feeling the shine has worn off the diamond?"

Vivien chuckled as she glanced up at her servant. The girl was very bright, really. "Yes. An apt metaphor."

"I suppose you could..." Rachel trailed off, her lips pursed in concern.

Vivien sat up straighter. "I could what?"

"Well..." Rachel glanced down at her. "You could...stop."

Vivien's lips parted. Dear God, she had never considered that. Being Vivien Manning, Courtesan Extraordinaire had become her everyday life. But what if it wasn't? What would she do if she was just...*herself?*

"I've spoken too plainly," Rachel fretted, wringing her hands in her lap. "I'm sorry, Miss Vivien."

Vivien glanced over at her. "No, no, Rachel, not at all. I asked you for your counsel and you have given that to me. In more ways than I could have imagined when I invited you up here to forget my feelings. But I think you may be…correct, though I cannot believe I am saying so."

Truly she could not, but when she said those words out loud, they gained even more power. She tingled with them, more excited by the idea of walking away from this life than she had been by any lover in…well, since her last protector.

"Correct?" Rachel whispered.

She nodded. "Having you say these things has made me realize I don't *want* to do this anymore. To be this person anymore. I—I want a new life. Where I can start over."

Rachel stepped back until she bumped the settee arm with her backside. Her voice trembled as she whispered, "Miss Vivien…"

"Oh, please don't look so forlorn!" Vivien burst out. "I could not just disappear in a moment's time. I wouldn't do that. I need time to arrange for a new home, a new name, to make sure my servants were taken care of. And have you ever known me not to make my exit spectacular?"

Rachel laughed. "No, miss. You have always sparkled on your way into any room and on your way out. No one could miss your entrances or exits."

"And this shall be no different." Vivien clapped her damp hands together as her mind raced. "If this Season is to be my last, I shall make it such a Season that when I disappear, my legend will be whispered of for years to come."

Her servant's eyes widened and then a grin began to spread across her pretty face. "Miss Vivien, that could be…"

"Spectacular?" She laughed. "Oh yes. I very much intend it to be so. Now run into my dressing room and fetch a piece of paper and a quill. I have much to plan if this is to truly end my reign as Master of the Mistresses!"

The girl giggled as she rushed into the other room and brought back the items Vivien had required. She sank back into the tub and pondered. Oh, there were many lists to be written. Things to do. Money to spend. Homes to find. Ways to remain anonymous in whatever new place she arrived in.

But right now she had an entirely different list on her mind.

"At the top of the paper, write 'Loose Ends to Tie Before Departing London,'" she ordered.

The scratch of the pen made her smile as she thought of everything she wanted to do to make this last Season oh-so-memorable.

"First, celebrate my friends." She sighed as she thought of them. She had many acquaintances and clinging hangers-on, but there were only a few people she counted as true friends. Mariah and Lysandra were chief amongst them. Before she vanished, she wanted them to know how much they were appreciated and loved.

"Yes, miss," Rachel said. "Second?"

"Destroy someone evil," she said with a frown. There were many she could count in that number. She had always remained silent to protect her reputation, but without those bonds? Oh, she could destroy. "And third, protect someone good."

"I like those," Rachel said as she scribbled away.

"I rather do myself. Fourth, indulge in pleasure." She hesitated. "I realize that may seem silly coming from me, since that is the life I intend to leave. But once I am a respectable woman with a new name, I do not think I shall have the freedom to carouse as I can do now. I shall have to get it all out of my system."

She glanced up to find Rachel blushing as she wrote down the item. But she was also smiling.

"Fifth?"

"Give away that which I do not need," Vivien said.

There was much that fit that description. She had amassed a great deal of wonderful things, some of which would come with her wherever she ended up, some would be sold. But if she could bestow some happiness from her things on to deserving parties, she wanted to do so.

"Sixth," she continued, "Enjoy London. For I do not think I will be able to return until age has changed my face enough to make me unrecognizable."

"Oh, Miss Vivien," Rachel sighed. "I do not like to think of that."

She shrugged, though in truth she didn't like to think of it either. London had been her home for ten years. It had given her wealth and solace after a painful childhood. She would miss it.

And yet, she did not feel a desire to alter her course.

"Number seven, I wish to revisit the past."

She hesitated as Rachel scratched out her sentence on the list. There were many things left unresolved in her past. Things that she dreaded facing. But she would. Once and for all.

"And while I am pursuing number seven," she said with false lightness. "I would also like to complete number eight and settle a debt."

"A debt?" Rachel said in surprise. "I beg your pardon, ma'am, I did not realize you were a gambler."

Vivien barked out a laugh. "Oh, all mistresses and courtesans are gamblers, my dear. But that isn't the kind of debt I mean."

No, she meant a debt to the man who had plucked her from a path of ruin and made her something more. She owed him something. She intended to repay that debt now.

"And finally, I suppose my final loose end will be to disappear," she said with a smile.

Rachel's hand faltered. "Disappear."

"Yes. That will lend the right twist to this grand gesture, I think. I shall vanish on the wind and leave the world gossiping."

Rachel slowly wrote her mistress's last loose end and then set the paper aside with a sad sigh. "Are you certain this is the course you wish to follow?"

Vivien hesitated. "I am not certain of much lately. I suppose that has been the cause of the malaise you have noticed. But of this course I am certain. And now, help me out."

Rachel moved to the edge of the tub with a towel in hand and helped Vivien step onto the floor. As she wrapped the towel around her mistress, Vivien sighed.

"I can dry myself. Go and finish whatever your normal morning routine is. I shall ring to be dressed in a few hours."

"Yes, miss," Rachel said with a quick curtsey.

"Oh, and Rachel?" she called out as the girl moved toward her door.

She turned back. "Yes?"

"I trust you, but I must ask you to be discreet. Please do not tell anyone, not even the other servants, of my plans. I will do so myself, when the time is right."

Rachel nodded. "Yes, miss. I will not speak a word of this. You may depend on me."

The girl slipped away. Once the door shut behind her, Vivien tucked the towel more firmly around her and moved to the list Rachel had abandoned on the seat. In her neat handwriting, the girl had marked out a plan for Vivien's explosive departure from the life she had been living.

And when she looked at that list, she thrilled at its nine points. And realized there was one missing.

One loose end she had never resolved. One loose end that haunted her daily, weekly, monthly.

She caught up the pen, dipped it in ink and added a final number to the list:

10. *Benedict Greystone.*

Order Now!

ALSO BY JESS MICHAELS

The Kent's Row Duchesses

No Dukes Allowed

Not Another Duke

Not the Duke You Marry

Theirs

Their Marchioness

Their Duchess

Their Countess

Their Bride (Coming January 2024)

Regency Royals

To Protect a Princess

Earl's Choice

Princes are Wild

To Kiss a King

The Queen's Man

The Three Mrs

The Unexpected Wife

The Defiant Wife

The Duke's Wife

The Duke's By-Blows

The Love of a Libertine

The Heart of a Hellion

The Matter of a Marquess

The Redemption of a Rogue

The 1797 Club

The Daring Duke

Her Favorite Duke

The Broken Duke

The Silent Duke

The Duke of Nothing

The Undercover Duke

The Duke of Hearts

The Duke Who Lied

The Duke of Desire

The Last Duke

The Scandal Sheet

The Return of Lady Jane

Stealing the Duke

Lady No Says Yes

My Fair Viscount

Guarding the Countess

The House of Pleasure

Seasons

An Affair in Winter

A Spring Deception

One Summer of Surrender

Adored in Autumn

The Wicked Woodleys

Forbidden

Deceived

Tempted

Ruined

Seduced

Fascinated

To see a complete listing of Jess Michaels' titles, please visit:

http://www.authorjessmichaels.com/books

ABOUT THE AUTHOR

USA Today Bestselling author Jess Michaels likes geeky stuff, Cherry Vanilla Coke Zero, anything coconut, cheese and her dog, Elton. She is lucky enough to be married to her favorite person in the world and lives in Oregon settled between the ocean and the mountains.

When she's not trying out new flavors of Greek yogurt or rewatching Bob's Burgers over and over and over (she's a Tina), she writes historical romances with smoking hot characters and emotional stories. She has written for numerous publishers and is now fully indie and loving every moment of it (well, almost every moment).

Jess loves to hear from fans! So please feel free to contact her at Jess@AuthorJessMichaels.com.

Jess Michaels offers a free book to members of her newsletter, so sign up on her website:
http://www.AuthorJessMichaels.com/

facebook.com/JessMichaelsBks
instagram.com/JessMichaelsBks
bookbub.com/authors/jess-michaels